LOOK OUT

Book 2

Rebecca Parkinson

Day One

© Day One Publications 2015

First printed 2015

ISBN 978-1846-25423-9

All Scripture quotations are from the **New International Version** 1984 Copyright
© 1973, 1978, 1984

Published by Day One Publications
Ryelands Road, Leominster, HR6 8NZ

TEL 01568 613 740 FAX 01568 611 473

email—sales@dayone.co.uk

UK web site—www.dayone.co.uk

Printed by TJ International

Illustrations by Angela Allen

Dedication

For Alan, the original Archie's brother!

CONTENTS

Chapter 1

AWAY WE GO!

Archibald Edwards carefully scanned his bedroom with his binoculars, checking that he hadn't forgotten anything vital that would be needed for the next few days. He paused to look at Terry, his toy tarantula dangling menacingly on a piece of elastic suspended from the ceiling, and let out a loud sigh. He could think of lots of adventures he could have with Terry at his grandparents' house ... but he didn't dare! Due to the trouble Terry had caused in the past, Mum and Dad had banned Archie from taking Terry out of his bedroom, never mind out of the house!

"Are you ready yet, Archie?" Dad's voice boomed from the ottom of the stairs. "We need to get going if we're going to s the traffic."

chie grabbed his toy cockroach, gave an apologetic wave ·y and ran downstairs.

·ly smell wafted across the hallway and Archie ' his jog into the kitchen where his mum was just ,oked breakfast on the table.

'm, you're the best!" Archie announced, giving ·ug before launching himself into the chair at the iust as his little sister did the same.

"I was here first," squealed Molly.

"You were not!" Archie snapped, knowing that he had little chance of winning this argument as he was actually sitting on top of Molly.

"But you're sitting on me!" Molly continued. "So how can you have got here first?"

Archie saw Mum turn round and open her mouth; she was looking cross. He was going to have to act quickly.

"Good question, Molly," he said with a smirk. "But ..." he continued, "... not all questions can be answered. In Sunday school last week Johnny said that there are some things that only God will ever know. Isn't that right, Mum?"

"Well yes ..." Mum began.

"There you are, Molly," Archie interrupted. "Mum agrees. Now move!"

"But I didn't say ..." Mum began again.

"You agreed," repeated Archie, "that God knows what happened here even if we don't."

"But we do know," argued Molly. "You sat on me and my legs are nearly flat!"

Dad appeared in the doorway.

"Archie, move!" he ordered rolling his eyes. "And please don't have these sorts of silly arguments while you're staying with Grandma and Grandad this weekend."

"Don't worry," Archie answered with a grin, sliding into the chair next to Molly's. "Grandma and Grandad will have enough silly arguments to keep us happy all weekend—we won't need to have any of our own!"

Mum sat down at the table smiling.

"They do agree sometimes," she said rather unconvincingly. "Just not very often."

Archie and Molly grinned at each other. They loved going to stay with their grandparents. Grandma and Grandad lived in a big house in a small town about an hour's drive away. Archie enjoyed spending time making things with Grandad and helping him in the garden. Molly particularly looked forward to the amount of sweets Grandad let her eat. She was also very fond of their two pets: Kitty, a small, furry black cat who liked nothing better than to cuddle up next to Molly to be stroked, and Goldie, a goldfish who was ten years old, which is very old for a fish!

"Two whole two days with them!" sighed Molly, looking like her greatest dream was about to come true.

"Come on!" shouted Archie jumping up. "Let's go!"

Chapter 2

GRANDAD'S MACHINE

"**O**uch!"

Archie squealed for the sixteenth time on the journey.

"Molly, why on earth did you pile all your toys up on the back shelf?" he moaned, picking jigsaw pieces off his knee. "It's bad enough having to be squashed in next to all your Barbies, never mind being knocked out every time Dad brakes."

"Grandma asked me to bring some toys with me," Molly replied, pulling a face.

"Not this many," Archie grumbled. "Not a whole toy shop full of them!"

"Ouch!"

This time a packet of felt pens landed on his head and scattered over the back seat.

"Well, Grandma asked me to and Mum said I could, so there," Molly answered rather rudely.

"Mum!" Archie yelled. "Molly's being rude again."

"Mum!" yelled Molly at the same time. "Archie's being mean!"

"Stop it, you two," Mum ordered. "Archie, please remember that you are the older one so try to act like it!"

Archie screwed up his nose and turned to look out of the window. It wasn't fair. It was always him who got into trouble.

Whether it was at home or at school he always seemed to be in the wrong place at the wrong time. He let out a huge sigh and watched as his breath steamed up the cold window. Then he leant forward so that the tip of his nose touched the fogged up glass and spent the rest of the journey drawing different pictures with the end of his nose.

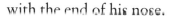

They were almost at Grandma and Grandad's house when Mum began her list of instructions.

"Now Archie," she said. "Make sure you behave yourself … Make sure you look after Molly …"

"Yes, Mum," Archie interrupted, rolling his eyes. "I'll be good even if Molly isn't."

Molly stuck out her tongue.

"And make sure you offer to help Grandma with things like shopping or cooking or whatever you can …" Mum continued.

"But I thought we were meant to be having a holiday …" Archie began.

Mum ignored him.

"Oh yes," she continued, turning round in the front seat to hand Archie a notebook. "Remember you've got to write a diary for two days for your holiday homework."

"Awwww, Mum," Archie groaned, his last shred of excitement rolling away.

"Can't I do it later in the week? I just want to enjoy being here, not think about school."

"It would be good to get it out of the way," Mum answered quietly. "And I'm sure Grandma would like to help you."

Dad winked at Archie in the mirror.

"I thought you'd want to impress your new teacher," he said smiling.

Archie shrugged his shoulders. It was so unfair to get homework in the holidays and he couldn't really imagine that a diary written by him could impress anyone—especially not a teacher!!!

"You can do it on the computer," Mum continued, trying to make him feel slightly better. "Grandma's got a new one. And you can add photographs as well."

"Here we are," announced Dad, pulling into the driveway and switching off the engine.

As Archie climbed sadly out of the car, Grandad appeared in the doorway shouting,

"They're here!" so loudly that the whole street must have heard.

Grandma came running round from the back garden and gave Archie a hug which left him gasping for air, while Grandad picked up Molly and spun her round so high that Dad had to quickly duck out of the way.

"Oh Archie," said Grandma seeing Archie's sad face. "What's the matter? You don't look like your usual smiley self."

"He's got to do his homework," smirked Molly. "Lots of writing!"

"I've got to write a diary," mumbled Archie miserably. "Talk about spoiling a holiday; Mum's just reminded me."

"Tell you what, love," said Dad, "you can use my camera and take loads of photos."

"And he can use the computer," said Mum, still trying to cheer him up. "It doesn't have to be written by hand."

"YES!!!" Grandad shouted suddenly, punching the air with his fist and making everyone jump.

"Yes! Yes! Yes!" he added, grinning at Grandma. "I told you it would be useful!"

"He's got a new toy," Grandma explained, seeing everyone's confused faces. "He went out shopping on his own and came back with a machine that types words straight into the computer when you speak into it."

Archie's face lit up.

"And you said I'd never use it," Grandad sang, dancing in front of Grandma like an excited child.

"I said you'd never be able to use it," corrected Grandma, rolling her eyes. "And your first try wasn't exactly a success was it?"

Grandad pulled a face at Archie.

"No," he said quietly, looking down at the floor.

"What happened, Grandma?" Molly giggled, recognising the

look on Grandad's face which usually meant there was going to be a funny story.

"He sent an email to our friends Joshua and Naomi," explained Grandma. "But he hadn't read the instructions which said you had to train the machine to recognise your voice before you used it, or else it would pick up every little sound that you made! And he sent the email without reading it first or showing it to me! Anyway let's get a cup of tea and I'll show you what he sent—I've never been so embarrassed in all my life!"

"Get ready for a laugh," Grandad whispered in Archie's ear as they followed Grandma inside. "I forgot it recorded everything, even my sneezes! But we'll get it sorted and you'll be able to speak your homework … and you've never had any problem speaking!"

As soon as Grandma had placed a tray of drinks and cakes on the table, she shuffled through a pile of papers and handed a printed sheet to Mum who began to giggle as she read it out loud. Archie peered over her shoulder.

Deer Josh you are and Neigh oh me,
Wee really enjoyed seeing ewe on chews day.
Atchoo! Atchooo! Oh deer, I need to get a tissue. Is a bell,
can you get me a tissue? Where are you? Oh well, I'd better
get my own. That's better. Don't want my nose running all
over the computer. Ur yuk, what a mess that would be. Now
where was I up to?

Atchooooooo! Oh no, not again. I must be getting a cold. Hope Is a bell doesn't get it.

Oh yes. Would you be free to come round for a meal next fry day?

Uuuuuuuuurrrrrrrrrrrrrrrrrrrrrrrrrrrrrrrrrr

Excuse me, that was a good burp. Archie would have been proud of that one.

Anyway, it would be lovely if you could come. If not, then maybe we could ketchup again sometime soon.

Love from
Hairyund Is a bell

Mum wiped her eyes.

"You'll have to stop talking to yourself, Dad," she giggled. "We always said it would get you into trouble sometime."

"Did you really send it, Grandad?" Archie asked, a huge grin spreading across his face.

"'Fraid so," Grandad muttered. "Grandma made me ring up to apologise."

"Mum's always making me do that," said Archie. "Well at least apologise … she doesn't usually make me ring up. She says you should say sorry face to face."

"Well don't tell your Grandma that," said Grandad looking horrified. "Or next time she'll be marching me round to Joshua and Naomi's house!"

"Who is Hairyund?" asked Molly innocently. "And why is he a bell?"

Archie rolled his eyes.

"Harry and Isabel," he explained in a voice that pointed out that he was far cleverer than his little sister. "Grandad and Grandma's proper names."

Molly still looked confused.

"Why do they have two names?" she asked. "Do I?"

"You have loads of names," he said, grinning mischievously. "Molly, grandchild, sister, daughter … annoying … pain …"

"Archie …" Mum warned, frowning at him.

Molly still looked confused.

"We need to go," announced Dad, standing up before Molly and Archie could begin an argument. "Both of you be good and look after Grandma and Grandad. We'll see you on Wednesday at lunchtime."

"Have a lovely time," added Mum. "I hope the homework goes well, and remember to help Grandma!"

"They'll be fine," promised Grandad. "Come on Archie let's go out and say good bye and then we can get this thing trained to recognise you!"

Chapter 3

THE SPACE GIRL

"I can't believe this!" repeated Archie for the fifteenth time. "It's the most amazing thing in the world!" Grandad smiled.

"Can you tell that to Grandma?" he asked. "She doesn't seem to believe me!"

"*Heeeeeellllllllllllllllllllllllllllllllloooooooooooooooooooooo,*" Archie watched as the words appeared on the screen in front of him.

"*Mooooooooooooooooooooooooooooooooo.*"

"*Brrrrrrrrrrrrrrrrrrrrrrrrrrrrrr.*"

"*Diiiiiiiiiiiiiiiiiiiiiiiiiiiiinnnnnnnnnnnnnnnnnnnnnnnnnngggggggggggggg.*"

"*Poooooooooooooooooooooooooooooooooooooooooooooooo.*"

It had taken two hours of Archie reading words into a microphone to train the computer to recognise his voice. Now it seemed that he could say anything and it would appear like magic in front of him.

"*I don't like writing. I don't like homework. I have been here for two hours and I still haven't had a sweet.*"

Grandad laughed as, right on cue, Molly appeared beside him.

"Please can I have a sweet, Grandad?" she asked, giving the smile that usually got her whatever she wanted.

"Of course you can, love," Grandad answered, opening a

drawer and handing Molly such a huge bag of toffees that her eyes almost popped out of her head.

Molly took the bag and darted for the door.

"She's not allowed those!" Archie screeched, as Molly made her escape. "Mum says they'll pull her teeth out and she'll need false ones like yours."

"Whoops," said Grandad guiltily, leaping up to search for Molly who had disappeared from sight.

Almost immediately they heard a loud, strange, gurgling noise coming from the dining room.

"She's in there," shouted Archie.

After that everything happened quickly. Grandad and Archie dived through the door to find Molly standing in the middle of the room making a funny noise and dribbling out of the corners of her mouth.

At the same moment Grandma ran out of the kitchen and screamed at the top of her voice, "She's choking!" (Later Archie pointed out that that 'choking' was a total exaggeration—more like she had crammed so many sweets in her mouth that she couldn't speak!)

Grandad sprang over to Molly and banged her on the back. When it didn't make any difference to Molly's gurgling noise, he grabbed her legs and, with one dramatic swing, turned her upside down. Grandma rushed forward and whacked her on the back again. Molly coughed and the sweets fired out of her mouth like bullets from a machine gun. They zoomed through the air and landed with a loud splash in the fish bowl, narrowly missing Goldie the fish.

Grandad put her down, and Molly immediately let out an almighty wail.

"My fish, my sweets!"

She dived forwards, unfortunately tripping over Kitty who was having a wash in the middle of the floor. The cat let out a blood-curdling yelp and Molly followed the sweets by rocketing headfirst into the fish bowl! The force of her landing was so terrific that when she stood up the bowl was firmly wedged on top of her head, its rim just touching the tips of her ears and neatly in line with her eyebrows. She looked like a tiny space man; however, the fact that Goldie was still swimming frantically in the water sloshing around on top of Molly's head made it clear that she wasn't really from outer space!

Molly continued wailing, "My 'ead's cold! Where's my fish; where's Goldie; where's my sweets?" while Grandad and Grandma tried to decide what to do.

"I wish my friends could see this," Archie mumbled, trying hard not to laugh and suddenly having an idea.

"I'll get the camera," he announced running up stairs. "Dad told me to take lots of pictures. Whatever you do, don't get the bowl off till I come back down!"

"You can't show your mum this!" Grandma bellowed behind him. "She'll never let you stay here again!"

When Archie returned downstairs Grandma was in the kitchen making a cup of tea as she always did if there was a crisis.

Molly was sitting on Grandad's knee suggesting that maybe they should all pray because, if God could rescue Daniel from the lion's den, then he could definitely rescue her from having a fish bowl stuck to her head.

"We can't get it off," Grandad explained, pulling a concerned face at Archie. "I've rung the fire brigade and I'm just explaining to Molly that sometimes God uses other people to help us with our problems."

"He does," agreed Archie, sitting down next to Molly, feeling slightly surprised that he felt sorry for her. "Once when I didn't want to eat some horrible, mushy fish thing at school dinners I prayed that God would help me. Just then one of the teachers appeared carrying Jamil's trainers and asked him to go out to practice tennis on the yard. Jamil was sitting next to me so he took his shoes off and left them on the floor …"

"You didn't …" Grandad began to speak.

Archie!—Look Out

"I did …" continued Archie. "… I put the fish in his shoe and walked out of the hall carrying them. Unfortunately, on the way out the same teacher smelt the fish and I got into trouble … but at least I got out of eating it! I told Johnny my Sunday school teacher about it and he said that I shouldn't really have done it but God can use any situation in an amazing way!"

"What happened to Jamil's shoes?" asked Molly.

A guilty expression came over Archie's face.

"Jamil went home in his trainers and unfortunately I went to play football and forgot to take the fish out of his other shoes until the next day. His shoes smelt so bad that his mum thought he had a medical problem and took him to the doctors."

"I don't think you'd better tell me anymore," Grandad said, glancing round to check that Grandma hadn't been listening. "Why don't you go and wait outside for the fire engine?"

Archie quickly jogged outside and waited by the gate. He soon heard the siren and waved as the firefighters jumped off the machine.

"The space girl's in here," he announced, leading them inside.

"Oh dear!" said one of the firefighters when they saw Molly. "Got yourself a bit stuck there, haven't you? My name's Jim. What's yours?"

"I'm not sure," muttered Molly looking confused. "It could be Molly or grandchild or sister or daughter …"

"It's Molly," interrupted Archie before Molly could embarrass him.

"OK, Molly," said Jim gently. "We'll have you out of there in no time at all."

"Bet you've never seen this before!" said Archie, settling down on a chair and watching with interest. "Dad's a firefighter and he tells us loads of stories ... but I've never heard of this!"

Jim laughed.

"No, I've not seen this one before but we've seen some pretty funny sights recently. Last week we had a man with his finger stuck in a plughole and the week before we had to rescue a lady who got her big toe stuck in the tap, whilst having a bath!"

"Oh!" said Molly, her eyes almost popping out of her head.

"I bet she wouldn't want me taking pictures," Archie giggled, secretly taking another photograph of Molly.

"No, I don't suppose she would," Jim agreed. "Hold still now, Molly, we'll soon have you sorted."

It didn't take long for the firefighters to remove the bowl from Molly's head, although, in the end they did have to break it—the bowl that is, not her head! Archie managed to take 47 photographs without Molly noticing, and soon the firefighters were eating a huge pile of cakes that Grandma had produced from the kitchen. Molly cuddled up on Grandad's knee, woefully watching Goldie who was swimming extra slowly round Grandma's see-through jug.

"Do you think he'll die?" Molly asked Grandad, once the firefighters had left.

Grandad shrugged his shoulders. "I don't know, love," he said gently. "We'll just have to wait and see."

Monday, 3:58pm—The start of Archie's holiday diary:
Wow! This machine of Grandad's is amazing!! First I had to read loads of words into it so it got to recognise my voice. At first I thought you had to speak slowly, so I kept getting words like 'heeeeellllllllllllllllllllooooooooooooooooooooooooo' appearing on the screen. But now I'm used to it, it's brilliant. Grandad made me have a go at burping and it looked like this 'uuuuuuuuuuuurrrrrrrrrrrrrrrrrrrrrrrrrrrrrrr!'
Waved Mum and Dad off. Spent ages teaching this machine to recognise my voice. Molly fell in the fish bowl. It got stuck on her head with the fish still in it. Funniest thing I've ever seen—can't wait to show my friends the pictures! Fire engine came and a firefighter called Jim smashed the bowl. Molly and the fish are both OK but Goldie is swimming very slowly. Going out now to help Grandad in the garden. Wow—that took me about 45 seconds—would have taken me about three hours to write it—wow, wow, wow, wow!

Chapter 4

MRS PILKINGTON'S CAT!

"Can I help?" Archie asked, running over to Grandad, who was pulling the lawnmower out of the shed.

"You can take this round to the front lawn," Grandad answered gratefully. "I'll be there in a minute."

Archie was just passing the little sandpit where Molly was happily playing when a head popped up over the hedge.

Archie recognised Mrs Pilkington immediately. She was one of Grandma's best friends, although, they couldn't have looked more different. Grandad called her 'Grandma's posh friend' because of the way she talked, but everyone liked her, even if she did tend to turn up at the worst possible moments. Mrs Pilkington was the sort of lady who always wore loads of make-up, especially bright red lipstick, and she always wore unusual hats, often with a matching handbag. Today was no different. Despite the bright sunshine, Mrs Pilkington was wearing a black furry hat that reminded Archie of a picture he had once seen of people in Russia during the winter. She was carrying a matching black furry bag with a large red lily on each side of it.

"Hallo, Archie. Hallo, Molly," she said in her usual posh voice as she came in through the gate.

Molly jumped out of the sandpit and ran over to say hello. Mrs Pilkington's face filled with horror.

"MOLLY, WHAT HAVE YOU DONE TO YOUR HEAD?"

Archie looked at Molly's head. "She looks like an angel whose halo fell down." He laughed. "It's the best bruise I've ever seen!"

"It does look quite amazing," said Grandad, walking into the front garden and frowning at Archie in a way that told him not to comment on the posh voice he was using. "Hello, Mrs Pilkington, do come in; Isabel's in the front room."

Mrs Pilkington sat down on the sofa and placed her hat on the cushion beside her. Molly soon moved to sit next to her, lifting the hat onto her knee and stroking its fur in different directions to make patterns. Archie perched on the arm of Grandad's chair, trying his best to look interested in the conversation. After ten minutes Grandad stood up.

"Would anyone like a cup of tea?" he asked, in a voice which sounded like he lived in a palace.

"Not another!" said Molly. "We'll be up all night weeing."

Grandad looked slightly embarrassed, pointed out that it was still a long time until bedtime and to Archie's relief asked if he would help him in the kitchen.

"What's with the posh voice?" asked Archie, as Grandad poured water into the teapot.

"Don't know really," Grandad answered, shrugging his shoulders. "I suppose the first time Mrs Pilkington came round I was trying to impress her, and now I daren't talk in a normal voice when she's around because she'll know I've been pretending for twelve years!"

Archie nodded his head.

"Last week in Sunday School, Johnny told us that he had once told his great-auntie that he liked her knitted jumper which had a picture on it of a bunny rabbit standing on one leg pulling a funny face and wearing a Christmas hat. He meant it as a joke, but she believed him, and she makes him one every year! He has to wear it on Christmas Day because she always goes to his house for lunch. Last year his girlfriend went for lunch, but he still had to wear the jumper. He felt really silly, and his girlfriend dumped him two  days later. His mum said it was because he forgot to buy her a Christmas present, but Johnny was certain it was because of the jumper. He said we should never pretend to be something that we're not, but that if we get it wrong and end up wearing a silly jumper we should remember that God looks on the inside of us, not at what we're wearing. He said it was a shame his girlfriend didn't know that!"

"Good advice," said Grandad, picking up the tray of teacups. "Can you take the rest of the stuff, Archie, and open the doors for me?"

Archie carried the small plates and a huge amount of cake into the lounge and put them carefully on the table, next to

Archie!—Look Out

Mrs Pilkington's hat, which Molly had placed there and was continuing to stroke gently. It was then that disaster struck!

Grandad entered the lounge carrying the tray of teacups. Suddenly, he stopped completely still, took a sharp intake of breath and shouted at the top of his voice!

"Kitty, you naughty cat, get down, get down, I said. Molly, you know that we don't allow the cat in here."

Everyone looked around the room stunned, their eyes searching everywhere for the naughty cat. Nobody could see her.

Grandad continued in a loud voice, "Mrs Pilkington, I'm so sorry. We don't allow our cat to climb on the table. Get down, Kitty, get down now!"

Suddenly, Archie realised what was happening. He opened his mouth to speak, but he was too late …

Grandad banged the tray down on the table and with one catastrophic wallop and a further furious cry of, "You naughty cat!" sent Mrs Pilkington's hat flying across the room, landing behind a chair in the corner.

Archie put his hand over his mouth to try to stop the giggles. There was a moment of silence as Grandad stared in horror at

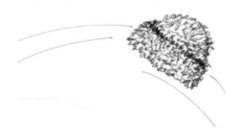

the chair, obviously waiting for a yelp from Kitty or for her to crawl out looking sorry. When nothing happened, he whispered anxiously, "I hope I haven't killed her."

He tiptoed over, knelt down, reached behind the chair and picked up the little furry object.

"It's OK, little cat," he whispered gently. "Grandad's not cross, but you know you're not allowed on the table."

Suddenly, Molly's little confused voice broke the silence.

"Grandma, why is Grandad cross with Mrs Pilkington's hat?"

At the same moment, Grandad realised his mistake and turned a brighter colour of red than a sunburnt tomato. Archie ran from the room and collapsed in a heap on the kitchen floor, tears running down his face.

Once Archie's giggles were under control, he wandered back into the lounge and found that Molly had helpfully smoothed out the fur on the hat. Glancing round to make sure no one was looking, he secretly pulled two small clumps of fur into points, making them look remarkably like Kitty's ears. Mrs Pilkington left soon after that. On her way out, she assured Grandad that she was not kidnapping Kitty and that it really was her hat, not the cat, sitting on top of her head! Archie saw the twinkle in Grandad's eyes as he noticed the ears. Unfortunately, Grandma noticed as well, but to Archie's relief she saw the funny side, especially when they looked out of the window and saw Mrs Pilkington's hat appearing to trot along the top of the hedge with its ears sticking triumphantly up in the air!

After tea Archie helped Grandad in the garden, while Molly

made some more cakes with Grandma before having an early
night.

Monday, 9:32pm—Archie's holiday diary:

*Wow! What an afternoon!! I've just climbed into bed.
It's been complete pandemonium! Wow, I could never have
spelt a word like 'pandemonium' if it wasn't for this brilliant
machine of Grandad's. I don't actually know what it means,
but Grandma's kept saying 'complete pandemonium'
over and over again all evening, so I think it fits in here!
Grandad's let me use his laptop in bed so I can 'write' from
under the duvet, as long as I talk quietly and Grandma
doesn't find out!*

*Mrs Pilkington came round and Grandad attacked her
hat thinking it was his cat, Kitty. Really funny! He knocked
it flying through the air like a bullet. You should have seen
Grandma's face! Anyway, Grandma seems to have forgiven
him! I don't think I've laughed so much ever.*

*Molly went to bed really early, but she kept coming
downstairs saying she couldn't get to sleep. After a bit I went
upstairs to tell her that I would tell Mum if she didn't stop
messing around, but she burst into tears and said her head
hurt and she was scared. I suddenly remembered a Bible
verse that Johnny taught us in Sunday school. It was from
Psalm 4 and said: 'In peace I will lie down and sleep, for
you alone, O LORD, make me dwell in safety.' I told Molly
that she didn't need to be scared because God was there all*

the time even when Mum and Dad weren't. That seemed to make her feel better, and she didn't come downstairs again. It actually made me feel really good that I helped her. (I might take that bit out of this diary in case Ben or Jamil read it!) After that the three of us watched a bit of TV, and Grandma made some supper. She had bought my favourite cheese, but I was only allowed to have a tiny bit, because she remembered that it used to give me nightmares when I was about two. Can you believe that? What's the point of buying your favourite cheese if you're not allowed to eat it? Sometimes, they still seem to think I'm a baby! Anyway, Grandad ate loads, so I hope he doesn't keep me awake screaming!

Going to sleep now. Hope tomorrow's as funny!

Chapter 5

IN THE MIDDLE OF THE NIGHT

Archie shot bolt upright in bed wondering what noise had woken him. His heart was pounding rapidly as he peered out into the darkness. He could see nothing unusual and was about to lie down when suddenly …

BANG!

"Ow! Ow! Wake up!"

Archie knew immediately it was Grandad's voice. He sprang out of bed and raced across the landing to Grandma and Grandad's room.

Grandad was lying wide awake in bed with Grandma very soundly asleep beside him.

"Are you OK?" Archie asked anxiously, looking round to see what could have disturbed him. "What's all the noise?"

From the light of the street lamp outside Archie saw a wide grin spread across Grandad's face.

"Watch and listen," he whispered. "Do you remember Grandma once telling you how she had always wanted to be a swimmer or diver in the Olympics?"

Archie nodded. Grandma would often say that when she took them swimming to the local pool. It always made them laugh because actually she couldn't swim at all.

"Well," Grandad continued, "she'll never admit it, but

sometimes cheese makes her dream, and I think that's what she's doing now!"

As if she'd heard what Grandad was saying, Grandma turned suddenly onto her stomach and began to move her arms and legs in circular motion, her feet narrowly missing Grandad each time.

"I wasn't so lucky with the first few kicks," he whispered. "That's probably what woke you up … it really hurt!"

"What is she doing?" Archie giggled.

"Swimming the breaststroke," replied Grandad. "Just you wait for the front crawl!"

Right on cue, Grandma began to windmill her arms round and round, more like helicopter propellers than the front crawl. Grandad received three hard blows to the stomach in quick succession. He jumped out of bed as Grandma's legs began to kick wildly up and down.

"Look out, Archie, she's going to take off!" Grandad yelled, a huge grin on his face.

Suddenly, without warning, Grandma sprang on to her feet and stood on the end of the bed. She stretched her arms up into the air as high as they would go, placed her hands together and bent her knees …

"She's going to dive!" bellowed Grandad in horror.

Grandad dived first, catching Grandma in a wrestling hold and pulling her onto the bed. Automatically, Grandma grabbed a book from her bedside table and walloped Grandad with it. As the book made contact with Grandad's head, Grandma woke up.

"What are you doing?" she asked Grandad. "Are you OK, Archie? I'm sorry if Grandad woke you up, love. I've told him cheese makes him do funny things; fancy him trying to wrestle me in the middle of the night! I was having a lovely dream about the Olympic Games, and now he's spoilt it! Sorry, Archie. I'm going to stop him watching those ridiculous wrestling programmes!"

Grandad smiled feebly.

"I think we'll explain in the morning," he whispered to Archie, yawning. "At least I'll have you to back up what I say!"

Archie wandered back into his room and climbed into bed. For some reason he didn't feel very sleepy, so he picked up Grandad's machine ...

Tuesday, 2:46 am—Archie's holiday diary:
What an eventful night so far!

Cheese should be banned from Grandma's menu! Can't wait till we see Grandma's face when we tell her in the morning! It's hard to believe that Grandma doesn't know how to swim because the strokes she was doing on the bed were brilliant! I know she can't though, 'cos one year we were on holiday at the beach and Grandad got Grandma to lie in one of those huge inflatable rings. She looked really funny because she was almost folded in half with her bottom stuck down the hole. Grandad floated her around in the water for a while, but then Molly shouted to him and he forgot about Grandma. She floated out to sea and eventually had to be rescued by a man in a motor boat. The best bit was that Grandad didn't know what had happened so just waved at her as she went past in the boat! He was in big trouble.

Anyway I'd better try to get to sleep … nniiiiiiiiiight nnnnnniiiiiiiiiiiiiiiiiigggggggghhhht.

Chapter 6

GRANDAD'S BOTTOM!

"**I** know that you'll both have planned a story about what happened last night," Grandma warned as soon as Archie appeared downstairs on Tuesday morning. "Your Grandad says I was going to dive off the bed … as if I'd do that!"

Archie sat down at the table next to Molly as Grandad walked into the room.

"Have you seen my bruise?" he asked with a grin, moving his fringe to show a tiny mark on his head.

"Oh Grandad," said Molly sympathetically. "How did you get yours?"

Grandad looked at Molly's multicoloured head and smiled.

"A little accident by your Grandma," Grandad explained. "Nothing so exciting as the way you got yours. Grandma sort of dropped a book on my head."

Grandma looked at him gratefully.

"Well, at least we match now!" said Molly eagerly. "We look like twins."

Grandma placed a pile of bacon sandwiches on the table.

"What would you like to do today?" she asked. "I've got a bit of shopping to do, but apart from that we've nothing planned."

"Do you need any help?" Archie asked, remembering what his mum had told him.

Grandma looked rather surprised.

"Wow, Archie, thank you," she said. "Sometimes I forget that you're growing up. If you don't mind, I would love a bit of help carrying the shopping. Maybe Molly could go to the park with Grandad and we could meet them there on the way home."

Archie immediately regretted his offer and was about to try to make an excuse when Molly let out an enormous wail.

"Grandma, your bash on Grandad's head has made his teeth fall out!" she shrieked, pointing to Grandad's teeth which were momentarily attached to his bacon sandwich and were dangling in mid-air.

Grandad made a grab for them, but he wasn't quick enough, and they clattered noisily onto his plate.

"Oh look, they're smiling at us," announced Archie in delight.

Molly was becoming hysterical, and Grandma quickly pulled her onto her knee as Grandad pushed the teeth back into his mouth.

"It's OK, Molly," Grandma explained. "Sometimes, when people get older, they have to get false teeth. That's why it's important to look after your teeth when you're younger. That's why your Mum always says that you shouldn't eat too many sweets and you should brush your teeth well at night."

"Johnny told us that just before his girlfriend dumped him he'd told her that her teeth were like sheep that had just been washed," Archie announced. "Apparently, he was trying to impress her with a quote from the Bible … it didn't work!"

"Why would you have a sheep in your mouth?" Molly asked, looking slightly ill at the thought.

"I don't know," said Archie shrugging his shoulders. "I'm only saying what Johnny said. Apparently, it's part of a song that King Solomon wrote in the Bible."

"Well, I don't want mine to fall out, whether they look like a sheep or not," Molly said sadly. "Can I get down from the table?"

Grandma nodded, and Molly wandered slowly out of the room.

"Poor little thing," said Grandma, watching her go. "She's having a traumatic couple of days."

Archie sat peacefully at the table eating his breakfast and listening to the radio until Grandma suddenly said, "Molly's very quiet."

Everyone looked at each other for a second.

"She's never this quiet," said Archie shaking his head.

Everyone sprang up like springs in unison shouting, "Molly!" at the tops of their voices.

Molly didn't answer, but Archie had a brainwave.

"The sweet drawer!" he shouted. "I bet she's there."

Sure enough, they found Molly sitting on the floor behind Grandad's desk looking like she was going to be sick. There were no sweet wrappers in sight, but clutched in her little hand was one of Grandad's large glue sticks, and there was evidence of glue all round her mouth.

"I just makin' sure my teef don't do what Grandad's did," she muttered, looking rather worried about what everyone would say.

"Oh Molly," panicked Grandma. "You can't glue your teeth in."

"We could put some wool on them," suggested Archie. "Then she would look like a sheep, and I could take a picture to show Johnny."

"Stop it, Archie," said Grandma, winking at him to reassure him that she wasn't cross. "Come on, Molly, let's get you upstairs and clean you up."

It took a long time to get Molly's teeth back to normal, but eventually she set off to the park with Grandad. Archie tried his best not to look sulky as he carried Grandma's bag to the shops. It didn't seem fair that Molly was at the park and he was shopping when it was Molly who had caused all the trouble that had happened so far! Shopping felt like a punishment for being good!

Thankfully, Grandma only needed to buy the ingredients for baking more cakes due to the huge amount the firefighters had eaten. To Archie's relief, they were soon on their way to the park, and to his surprise he felt really happy that he had helped, especially when Grandma bought him an enormous ice cream to say thank you!

"I hope we can find them," said Grandma, watching Archie attempt to lick the blob of ice cream that had attached itself to the end of his nose. "The park's massive. Anyway, we'll have a try."

There was absolutely no need for Grandma to worry. The moment they stepped through the park gates, it was perfectly clear where Grandad and Molly were!

Archie and Grandma looked at each other in horror as a tremendous wailing sound filled the air.

"That's definitely Molly!" Archie shouted.

They both set off running in the direction of the noise, eventually finding themselves at the back of a small crowd that

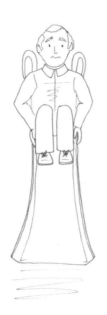

had gathered by the playground. The wailing was coming from somewhere in the middle, and they pushed their way past the people until they were standing at the base of a large slide.

Molly was sitting at the bottom of the slide, her dirty face streaked with tears.

"It's my fault. I made 'im do it and now Grandad's stuck," she wailed, pointing up the slide.

Sure enough, Grandad was firmly wedged about a third of the way from the top. He was rather red and was nodding to the crowd, assuring them, "I'm OK, no need to worry. You can all go home. When my wife arrives, she'll soon sort me out!"

It was perfectly clear that everyone in the crowd was determined to stay around to see what happened! It was also clear that Grandma had absolutely no idea what to do, although the look on her face suggested that she would happily leave Grandad there!

Archie climbed up the slide to investigate.

"The problem is …" he shouted down to Grandma and the interested crowd, "the problem is … his bottom is too big!"

A few children in the crowd started to snigger.

"He's got himself wedged," Archie continued. "The slide goes narrower at this bit. If we could shove him upwards, then we might be able to pop him out."

A few of the crowd stepped forward to help. Together they pushed on Grandad's feet and legs, but it was no use. Grandad didn't move at all.

"We once had a story in Sunday School," Molly announced, stopping her crying for a moment. "It was about someone called Jeremiah who got stuck down a well. A man got him out by wrapping rags round his armpits and pulling him up. Maybe we should try that."

Archie and a man from the crowd climbed the steps and

leant over the top of the slide, pulling at Grandad with all their strength, but it made no difference.

"I'm afraid there's only one thing we can do," Grandma said, rather reluctantly pulling out her mobile phone.

The return of the firefighters did at least stop Molly wailing.

"Oh good, it's Jim!" she shouted as soon as they arrived. "He's that one who rescued a lady from a bath," she added, smiling triumphantly at the puzzled crowd.

When the firefighters saw that it was Grandad stuck up the slide, they nearly split their sides laughing.

"Bit accident prone, you lot," chuckled Jim. "Good job they've got you to look after them," he added, nodding towards Archie.

Archie smiled and took a picture with Grandma's phone.

The rescue procedure was straightforward, except for Grandad's trousers still being attached to the slide once he had climbed down.

Enjoying the attention of the laughing crowd, Molly announced, "If you all come to our house now, Grandma will make you a nice cup of tea. She always does that in an emergency."

Grandma wrapped her coat round Grandad's waist, and they made their way slowly back to the house. To their surprise, two of the crowd were actually waiting on the doorstep.

"We haven't really come for a cup of tea," they explained. "We're from the local newspaper. We thought this would make a good story and just wondered if we could get a few details and maybe a couple of pictures."

Whilst Grandma was getting out her best china, the man took a photograph of Grandad and Molly, with their hair arranged in a very peculiar fashion to cover up all their bruises.

Molly did suggest that it might be a good idea to take a picture of Grandad's bottom, but to Grandma's relief the photographer said he didn't think that was necessary!

Playground Rebel Rescued

Tuesday, 1:22 pm—Archie's holiday diary:

What a morning! I couldn't have made this weekend up if I'd tried.

Grandad's teeth fell out at breakfast. Molly was really worried that hers might do the same, so she tried to glue hers in!! I had to help Grandma with the shopping, but at least I got a massive ice cream. Then Grandma heard Molly crying. I know people think that grandparents slow down as they get older; well, not Grandma! The moment she heard that wail, she was gone. Never mind her trying to get in the Olympic team for diving; she could have easily got in the Olympic team for the 100m sprint! Grandad was wedged in the slide, and the fire brigade had to rescue him! Can't believe they've rescued both Molly and him in the space of twenty-four hours!! Think Mum might go mad ... but at least it's not me for a change. I think Grandma wanted to keep it all secret, but now it's in the newspaper there's not much chance of that.

Chapter 7

OH DEAR, WHAT CAN THE MATTER BE?

After lunch Grandma announced that, following the excitement of the morning, everyone was going to remain at home for the rest of the day in the hope that no further incidents would occur.

Mum rang just as Archie shovelled his last chunk of cake into his mouth. Grandma had gone out of the room, so Grandad, despite Archie waving his arms and wildly shaking his head, passed the phone to Molly.

"Yes," answered Molly eagerly. "Yes, thank you, we're having a lovely time. I got a fish bowl stuck on my head, and Grandad got his trousers ripped off. And Grandma hit him over the head with a book and made his teeth fall out …"

Archie grabbed the phone.

"No, Mum," he insisted. "No, don't come and get us. We're fine. Yes, I am being good. No, I didn't put the fish bowl on Molly's head, and no, I didn't pull Grandad's trousers off … no, I didn't make his teeth fall out … I haven't done anything wrong … I even helped Grandma with the shopping … anyway, she's here now."

Grandma had hurried into the room, shaking her head more wildly than Archie had done earlier.

"Don't tell her anything," she hissed. "We don't want to spoil their break."

Archie handed her the phone and wandered into the lounge. Suddenly, he felt sad. He couldn't believe that Mum would assume all the trouble had been caused by him. He sat down on the sofa and put his head in his hands.

"Penny for your thoughts?" said Grandad, sitting down beside him.

Archie glanced up.

"I was just thinking," he began. "I was thinking that it's not fair that Mum thinks I would have caused all the trouble … but then I thought, actually it probably is fair really because usually it is me who causes it all!"

"It's not always you," said Grandad gently. "Quite often it's me!"

Archie smiled.

"It's just that sometimes I really want to be good and do the right thing," Archie continued, "but then something happens and I dive in and get myself in trouble. And now I've done it so many times that everyone assumes I cause every bit of trouble that ever happens. Johnny says that we should pray and ask God to help us, but when I pray, it never seems to make any difference. I sometimes think I'll always be in trouble till I'm a hundred!"

"You know, Archie," Grandad said softly, "when we ask God to change us, he hardly ever does it immediately. He does it bit by bit, and sometimes it can take a very long time. Do you remember the story of Peter in the Bible?"

"A bit," Archie answered. "I remember he chopped off a soldier's ear when they were trying to arrest Jesus."

"That's right," Grandad smiled. "He was always getting into trouble. If you remember, after Jesus had been arrested, Peter even said three times that he didn't know Jesus. He was always saying and doing the wrong things at the wrong time. Once he nearly drowned when he jumped out of a boat and tried to walk on water."

"Bit like me then," said Archie. "Always opening my mouth and putting my foot in it!"

"That's right," said Grandad smiling at him. "But Jesus thought he was worth all the trouble! In fact, out of all of Jesus' special friends, he became the leader! You're a great boy, Archie, and both me and Grandma have noticed a big difference in you recently."

"Harry!"

Grandma's voice broke into the conversation.

"We'd better go and see what she wants," Grandad said rather guiltily. "I don't think I'm quite out of trouble about the slide incident. She says I'm like a big child."

Archie laughed, thinking what a good description that was of Grandad but deciding not to say so.

"Harry," Grandma said as they walked into the kitchen, "it's such a lovely day I thought maybe you could tidy out the shed, seeing you've been going to do it for the past eight years. Maybe Archie could help you."

Grandad nodded meekly and led Archie outside to where Molly was peacefully playing in the sandpit.

"I'm going to get the sun lounger out for your Grandma," Grandad said, unlocking the shed door. "She likes lying out on that, and I need to make sure she's happy with me or we may not get any tea," he added, winking at Archie.

Grandad handed the lounger to Archie and disappeared back into the shed. Archie unfolded it quickly; it had given him an idea! He ran upstairs, rummaged in the bottom of his bag for his toy cockroach and sprinted back into the garden.

"Watch this," he said to Molly, placing the cockroach carefully on one end of the lounger. "Jamil taught me this!"

Archie sat down suddenly on the opposite end. The cockroach flew through the air, landing on the top of the wheelie bin.

"Can I have a go?" laughed Molly, jumping up.

For the next half hour, Archie and Molly played happily, setting up targets on the bin and firing a variety of objects at them, scoring points each time they knocked one down. They were so engrossed that they didn't realise that Grandad hadn't reappeared from the shed. Archie was just about to shout to check that he was OK when Mrs Pilkington opened the gate and walked up the driveway.

"Oh, hello again, Mrs Pilkington," Molly screeched at the top of her voice. "You don't have a cat on your head today."

Molly ran over and gave Mrs Pilkington a hug, looking up at her enquiringly.

"Do your teeth fall out like Grandad's?" she asked, gazing at Mrs Pilkington's mouth.

Archie hurried over to change the subject.

"I like your bag," Molly continued. "Can I tell you about what happened to Grandad at the park?"

Archie glared at her.

"Why are you staring at me?" Molly asked.

Archie ignored her.

"Hello, Mrs Pilkington," he said in such a polite voice that Grandad would have been proud. "I'll tell Grandma you're here."

Mrs Pilkington had only popped round to see if Molly was feeling any better after the fish bowl incident. She had brought her a present—the most hideous hat you could ever imagine. It was an exact replica of the one that Mrs Pilkington was wearing, bright fluorescent pink with a huge stripey rim and multi-coloured dots on springs sticking out from it. Molly loved it!

She threw her arms around Mrs Pilkington and wouldn't stop kissing her until Archie dragged her off. Mrs Pilkington actually appeared to be rather pleased, although Grandma looked horrified as she gazed at the huge streak of lipstick which, thanks to Molly's attack, now ran from Mrs Pilkington's lips all the way up to her left eyebrow.

In the heat of the moment, Grandma said, "Thank you so much for coming to see Molly. Will you stop for afternoon tea?"

Mrs Pilkington replied that she would love to, and Grandma asked Archie to take her round to the back garden to await refreshments.

Archie showed Mrs Pilkington to the best garden chair and placed a table next to her before sitting down carefully in the middle of the sun lounger and attempting to make polite conversation. Kitty came and cuddled down on one end of the lounger, and Mrs Pilkington removed her fluorescent hat, commenting that she was sure even Grandad couldn't mistake this one for any sort of animal!

Archie smirked and was just beginning to explain that Grandad wasn't usually as bad as that when a sudden cry of "Help, help, help!" ended the conversation.

Mrs Pilkington, Archie and Molly all peered round as the voice came again.

"Would anyone like to help me?" came the voice again, followed by loud banging which was obviously coming from the shed.

At that precise moment, the kitchen door opened, and Grandma appeared calling, "Harry, do you want a drink?"

"I'd love one!" Grandad shouted immediately. "But you'll have to pour it through the key hole. I'm locked in."

Grandma didn't have time to reply before Grandad burst into song:

Oh dear, what can the matter be,
I'm in the shed … can someone please rescue me!
I was stuck in the slide, now I'm stuck in the 'shed-ity',
Can you get me out of here?

Grandma let out a groan, but Molly looked delighted.

"Sing me another, Grandad," she shouted before anyone could stop her. Of course, Grandad obliged.

Oh dear, my little Mo-olly,
You must think your grandad's so si-i-lly,
Grandma will be so very cross with me,
If you cannot rescue me quick.

The look on Grandma's face made Archie giggle.

"Are you really stuck?" she asked, sighing wearily and raising her eyebrows to Mrs Pilkington.

"Certainly am!" Grandad replied. "Think you'll probably

have to get the fire brigade or find a screwdriver and take the door off yourself."

Grandma muttered that she would actually rather leave him in there for the rest of the day and that there was absolutely no way she was having the firefighters returning for the third time in 24 hours!

"I'll do it," said Archie jumping up, relieved that he could escape from a boring conversation.

While Grandma made the tea, Archie worked on the shed door, having first pushed a note under it to warn Grandad to keep his voice down as Mrs Pilkington was in the garden!

Grandma served tea and cakes and pretended everything was normal.

Mrs Pilkington had just taken her first sip of tea when there was an almighty bang as the shed door fell in, closely followed by an even mightier "Ow!" as it hit Grandad.

Grandad emerged looking dirty and hot. His bruise from the previous evening now had a twin on the opposite side of his head.

"Hello, how lovely to see you, Mrs Pilkington," he said politely as Grandma handed him a cup of tea.

Grandad glanced round. All the chairs were taken. He spotted the sun lounger and took a step backwards.

In a flash, Archie saw in his mind exactly what was going to happen—the lounger's ability to flip if a large weight was placed on one end ... and Kitty, who was sleeping quietly on the other end! He opened his mouth in horror, but no sound came out until it was too late! To him the next few seconds seemed to take place in slow motion.

Grandma, realising the same thing, managed to utter a desperate "Stop!"

But it was too late!

As Grandad muttered, "Oh, lovely, a cup of tea and a sit down," he transferred his entire body weight on to one end of the lounger.

Grandad banged to the ground with a loud thud. His cup flew out of his hand; the tea flew out of the cup and poured straight into the stripy brim of Mrs Pilkington's hat.

Meanwhile Kitty, making frightened mewing noises, was catapulted through the air like a rocket and landed with a splat on Mrs Pilkington's plate.

Mrs Pilkington screamed. Kitty jumped down with buttered scones stuck to all four paws like enormous shoes and a piece of buttered malt loaf attached to her bottom.

While Kitty tried to master the art of walking in shoes ten sizes too big, Grandma apologised again to Mrs Pilkington, and Archie laughed so hard he was certain his sides would split.

Molly offered two helpful comments. The first one was her offer to pull the piece of malt loaf off Kitty's bottom and return it to Mrs Pilkington's plate. This was quickly declined by both Grandma and Mrs Pilkington, who turned a funny shade of green. The second was to suggest that maybe they ought to ring the fire station to see if Jim could return to lift Grandad up again.

Everyone shouted "No!" very loudly to this suggestion, and Grandad leapt up quicker than a frog!

Mrs Pilkington left soon after. At the gate Archie heard Grandma apologise once more for the chaos, and he was surprised by Mrs Pilkington's reply.

"Don't apologise," she said in a quiet voice. "I don't think I've enjoyed myself so much since Fred died last year. You've no idea how lovely it is to be part of a family."

Archie saw the look on Grandma's face and somehow knew she was feeling the same as he was.

"Was Fred her husband?" Archie asked as Mrs Pilkington walked up the road.

"Yes, he was," Grandma said, nodding sadly. "Makes you realise how fortunate we are."

Grandad appeared round the corner.

"I'm sorry, love," he said to Grandma. "I didn't mean to embarrass you … again!"

To his surprise, Grandma placed her arm around his shoulders and planted a kiss on his cheek. Together they wandered inside, and Archie sat down on the grass watching them go. For some reason he had begun to think about something Johnny had said in Sunday School a few weeks previously. He had been telling them that the Church was like a big family, and he'd read a bit from the Bible that was talking about a body. It talked about how each bit of our body is different and how silly it would be for an eye or ear or hand to have an argument about which of them was the most important. Johnny had explained that children and old people, 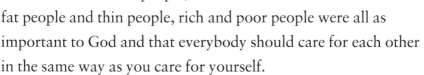 fat people and thin people, rich and poor people were all as important to God and that everybody should care for each other in the same way as you care for yourself.

Suddenly, Archie sprang up and ran inside.

"Grandma!" he shouted. "Can we ask Mrs Pilkington round tonight after tea to play some games?"

Grandma and Grandad looked at each other in amazement.

"If you'd like to," Grandma said smiling. "I'm sure she would be pleased."

Archie shot out of the door and up the road.

"Mrs Pilkington!" he bellowed. "Stop!"

Tuesday, 9:34 pm—Archie's holiday diary:

What a day! After Grandad spent the morning stuck in a slide, he spent the afternoon stuck in the shed! Funny, though ... although Grandad sang a rude rhyme in front of Mrs Pilkington and then fired Kitty into her afternoon tea, Grandma seems to have decided that she's not cross with him! Everything seemed to change when Mrs Pilkington said something that made me and Grandma realise that we have a lot to be grateful for! I even invited Mrs Pilkington back to play games tonight. You should have seen her face when I asked her! I don't think I've ever seen anyone look so happy! She knew some really silly games, and when we played charades she did the best impressions I've ever seen. Who would have thought she could be so funny? I guess it just goes to show that we look at older people and see what they look like on the outside and forget that inside they are still the same as they were when they were younger. As she went home, she squeezed my arm and told me my mum and dad must be so proud of me! I didn't like to correct her, but it made me feel good thinking that that's what she thought ... even if she's wrong!

Chapter 8

THE MONSTER!

It was three o'clock in the morning when Archie was woken up by a piercing scream and then a heavy thud which felt as if a huge animal had landed on his stomach.

For a moment, he was unable to breathe, and his heart pounded wildly.

It was only as the 'animal' uttered, "That monster is going to eat Grandma and Grandad," that Archie realised it was Molly who had landed on his middle and who was now clinging to him in terror.

Archie reached over and switched on the light.

"What on earth's the matter with you?" he asked. "There aren't such things as monsters."

"There are!" Molly continued to sob. "I heard them. They're in Grandma's room."

"Lie down here," Archie ordered. "Try to get back to sleep, and if we hear them again I'll go and have a look."

Molly cuddled down and began to doze off, while Archie teetered on the edge of the bed, trying not to fall out.

Then, suddenly, without warning, a terrible blood-curdling sound echoed through the room.

Archie sprang out of bed and Molly clung to him, shaking and repeating, "It's a monster, it's a monster."

For a moment Archie was too terrified to move. Molly was

right! The noise certainly seemed to be coming from Grandma and Grandad's room, and it did indeed sound as if a huge monster was roaring and possibly eating its prey, while the prey was desperately fighting for breath.

Archie shook his head, reminding himself that he was nine years old and that he knew monsters didn't exist, especially not in your grandparents' bedroom.

Tucking the duvet round Molly and instructing her to stay where she was, he tiptoed across the landing until he was standing outside Grandma and Grandad's bedroom door. The noise continued.

Archie slowly pressed down the handle and opened the door a tiny crack. Taking a deep breath, he peeped inside.

By the light of the street lamp shining through the curtains, Archie could clearly see Grandma sitting up in bed. From the look on her face, Archie at first thought she was terrified, but after a moment he realised she was actually furious!

Grandad lay flat on his back, his chest going up and down as the strange gurgling sound echoed from his vibrating cheeks. His teeth, glittering in a glass by the bed, looked as if they themselves were laughing at the sight.

Archie tiptoed back to his room.

"Molly, come here," he whispered. "There's nothing to be afraid of …"

Tightly grasping Archie's arm, Molly tiptoed towards the noise. This time Archie walked straight into the bedroom, and Molly gazed in amazement at Grandad before muttering in a worried voice, "Has Grandma hurt him again?"

"No!" Archie giggled. "He's snoring."

Archie led Molly nearer to the bed as Grandad's body suddenly gave an amazing quiver.

"It's like those jellies that Mum makes on our birthdays," Molly whispered.

Archie laughed as Grandad's body continued to wobble from side to side. Then suddenly his breathing quietened for a moment.

"Molly thought there was a monster in here," Archie whispered to Grandma, making the most of the silence.

"I wish there was," Grandma whispered. "Then I'd feed your Grandad to it and get a good night's sleep!"

"Can't you stop him?" Molly asked, turning her attention to the teeth that still seemed to be smiling.

"Well, sometimes this works," Grandma answered with a grin. She bent her leg, placed her foot under Grandad's back and pushed firmly. With a gargling splutter, Grandad heaved over onto his side and for a moment was completely silent. It was short-lived. Grandad obviously preferred to be on his back and slowly rolled again into his starting position, and the noise continued!

"We could wedge him," suggested Molly, "so that he can't roll back onto his back."

Archie looked at his sister in admiration.

"Great idea!" he said. "Go and get whatever you can find."

Molly hurried away and returned with three teddy bears, two beakers, the bathroom scales, a rug off her bedroom floor, six encyclopaedias and a large beanbag.

Grandma repeated her trick and with a quick flick of her foot rolled Grandad onto his side. Immediately, Archie piled Molly's complete collection behind Grandad until he was wedged firmly in place. At once the room was peaceful.

"Thank you," said Grandma, smiling at the children. "I just hope Grandad doesn't bulldoze the whole pile in the middle of the night."

"I know," Molly said suddenly.

Before they could stop her, she reached her little hand into Grandad's tooth pot, pulled out the grinning teeth and placed them on the bed very close to Grandad's bottom.

"What on earth are you doing?" asked Archie.

"Well," Molly explained, "if Grandad tries to roll onto his back, those teeth will bite his bottom and stop him!"

Both Grandma and Archie laughed.

"You're getting more like your brother every day," Grandma said, and to Archie's surprise, Molly grinned as if that was good news.

"Time for bed now," Grandma continued. "I don't know what your Mum and Dad will say when they hear about all of this!"

Wednesday, 2:22am—Archie's holiday diary:
Just climbed back into bed. Molly woke me up, scared that a monster was in Grandma and Grandad's bedroom. Turned out to be Grandad snoring! Molly had the idea of wedging him on his side and placing his teeth to bite his bottom if he tried to roll over onto his back! Grandma says Molly's getting more like me every day … funny thing is Grandma didn't seem too worried about that, and Molly looked very pleased. Can't really imagine anyone wanting to be like me. Anyway, Molly's asleep next to me. She didn't want to go back to sleep in her room in case a real monster came! She looks quite nice asleep, but she keeps spreading out so there's no room in the bed. Not sure I'm going to get much sleep!

Chapter 9

LOOK OUT!

Molly wouldn't lie still! She thrashed and kicked and, even worse, tried to cuddle Archie as if he were a teddy bear! Archie tried to move her, but she was even more awkward than Grandad had been and eventually he gave up, climbed out of bed, wrapped a blanket around himself and fell asleep on the floor.

Archie slept quite well until morning, when Grandad appeared in the room bringing breakfast in bed as a treat for their last day and as an apology for their disturbed night!

Unfortunately, Grandad was not expecting the bundle on the floor. Archie was woken by a loud shout. He opened his eyes to see Grandad flying through the air. Fortunately for Grandad, the bed provided him with a soft landing! Unfortunately for Molly, she was woken by the monster from the middle of the night flattening her!

"Get off, you monster!" she screamed so loudly that Olympic runner Grandma sprang into action, leaping up the stairs and sprinting into the room.

Unfortunately, Grandma wasn't expecting the bundle on the floor either and she too fell over Archie, landing on top of Grandad and giving her head a small bang on the wall.

Molly groaned and crawled out from underneath the heap with a piece of toast in her mouth.

"I think I am squashed, but Grandad, this toast is really nice!" she mumbled as Grandma and Grandad untangled themselves, discovering thankfully that neither of them were hurt in any way!

"You've got a bit of a red mark on your head, Grandma," Molly announced. "Now the three of us can be triplets with

matching head bruises! We'll need to give Archie one so we can all match!"

Grandma rolled her eyes and looked rather tired.

"I had hoped for a rather more normal day today," she sighed. "But it doesn't seem that we've got off to a very good start! Anyway, I'll go and make some more breakfast, but maybe it's best if we eat downstairs this time!"

Grandma trudged out of the room, and Archie sat on the edge of the bed next to Grandad.

"Cheer up," Grandad said, seeing Archie's face.

"I can't believe I can cause trouble before I even get out of bed!" Archie groaned.

"Actually, it was you getting out of bed that caused the trouble," Molly interrupted. "If you were in bed, Grandad couldn't have fallen over you!"

Archie stuck his tongue out.

"I was only being nice to you!" he said crossly. "Trying to let you sleep."

Molly looked guilty.

"Oh look!" she said, trying to change the subject. "See there where Grandad's cup of tea has splashed down the wall … it looks like a duck!"

Archie examined the patterns.

"That one's like a tree," he said, tilting his head to one side.

"And that one's like a washing line with underwear on it," Molly giggled.

Archie was just trying to make out the shape when Grandma shouted from downstairs.

Molly jumped up and left Grandad and Archie alone.

Grandad put his arm round Archie's shoulders.

"You know, Archie," he said gently, "over the last few days I've been watching you and thinking about something you said!"

"Oh no!" Archie gasped. "Was it rude? Am I in trouble? Was it about the fish in Jamil's shoe?"

Grandad laughed and shook his head.

"No, it was about that jumper that Johnny wears every Christmas."

Horror filled Archie's face.

"You're not going to ask Grandma to knit me one, are you?" he pleaded. "I really, really, really, really don't want one … I'd rather have a remote control …"

"Don't worry," Grandad interrupted. "I wouldn't dream of asking Grandma to knit you anything. No, I was thinking about how Johnny said that God looks on the inside of us."

"He didn't mean like our guts and things," Archie explained, wondering if Grandad had misunderstood.

"I know that!" Grandad laughed. "I was reading my Bible last night, and it was the part where God sent the prophet Samuel to choose the new king of Israel. God told him to go and meet a man called Jesse."

"That's a girl's name!" Archie interrupted.

Grandad ignored him.

"Jesse introduced Samuel to seven of his sons," he continued. "They were tall and handsome and looked wonderful. Samuel was certain one of them would be the future king … but God said 'no' to each one."

"Don't tell me that someone knits one of them a jumper with a rabbit on and they become the king!" Archie giggled.

"No," Grandad laughed. "Jesse announced that he had one more son, but he was only a young boy who was out in the field looking after the sheep."

"I know this story," said Archie. "It was David … the one who eventually killed Goliath."

"That's right," Grandad agreed. "But God said something very important to Samuel before he chose David. He said, 'People look on the outside of a person, but God looks on the heart.'"

Grandad gently tilted Archie's chin towards him so he could look into his eyes.

"You know, Archie," he said softly, "you may sometimes get into trouble. You may sometimes do things that are meant to be helpful but go wrong …"

"Like sleeping on the floor …" Archie added.

Grandad nodded and continued, "… But remember God can see what you are like on the inside. He knows how you helped Grandma with the shopping; he knows that you cared about Mrs Pilkington enough to ask her round last night; he sees how you cared for Molly enough to get out of bed and sleep on the floor. Even if other people only notice when you do things wrong … remember that God sees the good in you as well."

Archie thought for a moment.

"When Johnny said God has made us all different because it was like we were all one part of a body, we all had a laugh trying to work out which bit we'd be," he said seriously. "Ben said he'd be a wisdom tooth 'cos he was clever, Sarah said she'd be an ear because she liked listening to people's secrets … we said Johnny had better be a stomach so he could wear his jumper over it …"

Grandad waited. He could tell there was some point to Archie's rambling.

"Well, I couldn't really think that I could be any part of it," Archie said sadly, "because I'm not really good at anything at all! Although Ben did say that I could possibly be a nose 'cos sometimes I'm smelly!"

Grandad shook his head.

"Oh, Archie," he said smiling, "maybe Johnny should have told you what comes straight after the bit about the body in the Bible. The next bit says that more important than everything else is love."

"Yuk!" said Archie. "Glad he didn't tell us that!"

"Not soppy love," Grandad laughed. "Love that cares for other people … love that asks a lonely old lady round to play games … love that carries a shopping bag to make someone happy even when they'd rather be at the park … love that sleeps on a hard, cold floor …"

"You mean like just caring for people …"

Grandad nodded again.

"I don't always want to do nice things," Archie confessed.

"None of us always wants to do nice things," Grandad added. "That's why we have to ask God to help us to do the things that we know are right even though we want to do something else."

"Are you coming for breakfast?" Grandma bellowed up the stairs.

"I think the right thing to do just now would be to go and eat it!" laughed Archie.

"Couldn't agree more," said Grandad, as they raced each other down the stairs.

Chapter 10

FAMILY TRAITS

Wednesday, 10:21am—Archie's holiday diary:

Just had breakfast—yum. Mum and Dad coming for us at lunchtime, so doing this quick so we can play in garden for a while. Had such a good time here! Never laughed so much ever! Seems Grandad believes I'm not as bad as everyone else appears to think. Hope he tells Mum I've not caused all the brusises—Grandma's got one on her head now from falling over me on the floor! The three of them match. I'm feeling a bit left out!! Ha-ha … not really!

I don't want to go home. This has been the funniest time ever!

Gggggggooooooooooooooooooodddddddddd Bbbbbbbbbyyyyyyyyyyyyyyeeeeeeeeeeee.

Grandma's wish for a peaceful morning came true, and by the time Mum and Dad arrived, the table was set for lunch and Archie and Molly were playing happily in the garden.

"Mum!" screeched Molly as the car door opened.

Mum looked horrified when she saw Molly's bruise. Grandma had warned her on the phone, but that hadn't prepared her for the shock of Molly, who now looked like she'd fallen and dipped her head in a pot of purple paint.

"I hope you've both been good," Mum said as they sat down for lunch.

Archie and Molly nodded.

"They've been brilliant," said Grandad. "Couldn't have been any better."

"Grandad says I get more like Archie every day," Molly announced, obviously thinking that this was the sort of news Mum would like to hear.

Mum looked rather worried and opened her mouth to speak, but Dad interrupted her.

"Grandad tells me that Archie gets more like someone else in this room every day," he said, grinning round at everyone.

"Like Grandad?" guessed Molly.

"No," answered Dad.

Archie noticed that Mum was going slightly red.

Grandad nodded towards her.

"Not like Mum!" said Archie. "I bet she never did anything wrong when she was younger!"

Dad started to laugh.

"From the tales I've heard, she'd outdo you any day, young man!"

Archie's eyes nearly popped out of his head.

"I could tell you some stories about your mum," Grandad laughed, glancing at Mum to see if he'd be in major trouble if he did!

"Go on, Grandad," said Archie and Molly at the same time.

"Well, I remember once," Grandad began, "we went round to see an old auntie—Auntie Ann she was called. We used to go there quite often, and she would always insist that we stayed for tea. Anyway, on this occasion Auntie Ann appeared with five plates of food. Remember your Uncle Jack would have been there too—he's two years younger than your mum. Well, there were six cherry tomatoes on each of the plates along with the other food. Your mum looked at us in horror because none of us liked tomatoes; but both your mum and Jack knew that when they were out somewhere we would expect them to eat everything given to them. Well, the adults carried on talking, and the next time we looked, all your mum's and Jack's tomatoes had gone! We were so pleased with them. Even better, when Auntie Ann went out of the room, your mum asked if she could have ours off our plates."

Grandma suddenly laughed out loud.

"We thought she'd got a sudden liking for tomatoes," she giggled. "Parents can sometimes be so wrong about their children!"

"Anyway," Grandad continued, "all those tomatoes disappeared as well. We stayed talking to Auntie Ann for a while and then we said goodbye and climbed into the car. Grandma began to fuss about whether your mum needed to go the toilet or was going to be sick due to the amount of tomatoes she'd eaten when suddenly your mum rolled up her trouser legs! Your grandma screamed! It looked like her legs had some sort of terrible disease, but really her knee-length socks were stuffed full of cherry tomatoes!"

Everyone laughed, but Archie looked amazed.

"Look at Archie's face," Dad pointed out. "Wouldn't believe your mum would do that, would you?"

"What about this one," Grandad continued. "One day when your mum was about Molly's age, your grandma had made

spaghetti bolognese. Your mum refused to eat it—at least she ate the meat but wouldn't eat the spaghetti. We told her she was going to sit at the table until she had eaten it, even if that meant she sat there all day. At first she just sat still looking sulky but eventually, when we went back into the room, all the spaghetti had gone! We told her how proud we were of her and that was the end of it …

until she went to bed and Grandma went to close the kitchen door. Hanging over the handle was every bit of your mum's spaghetti!!"

"Mum!" shouted Molly, obviously shocked. "Even Archie wouldn't do that!"

Archie nodded.

"I might now!" he muttered, winking at Dad.

"Tell them about Mrs Scott's glasses," said Dad, enjoying watching Archie's face.

Grandad laughed.

"Your mum was about nine years old, like you are now, Archie. Grandma and I had gone out for the day and a friend of ours, Mrs Scott, had come to look after your mum and Jack. Jack had got a dart gun for Christmas. It had little sticks with suction pads on the end that stuck onto windows and walls if you hit them correctly. Anyway, for some reason your mum was cross with Mrs Scott that day, and when Mrs Scott told the children to tidy up ready for lunch, your mum got Jack's dart gun and fired it at her. It knocked her glasses off! She was very cross."

"Mum!" gasped Archie. "I don't think even I would do that. What happened?"

"I ran away," said Mum, taking up the story. "We had some fields at the back of the house. I ran out of the back door, jumped over the fence and sprinted across the field."

"Carry on," said Dad, as Mum stopped speaking. "Tell them the rest."

"Worst thing was," Mum continued, "Mrs Scott did the same thing … and even though I thought she was about 500 years old, she actually caught me!"

"I'm not surprised at that!" Archie said rather cheekily.

"I was in such trouble when Grandma and Grandad came home. Although I still think I heard Grandad laughing once I'd been sent up to bed."

Grandad looked guilty and nodded his head violently at Archie when no one was looking.

"You see, Archie," Grandad said, when everyone else had left the table, "your mum hasn't turned out too bad, has she, considering what a lot of trouble she caused when she was young."

Archie shook his head, still suffering from shock.

"You remind me so much of your mum," Grandad continued. "And when I've heard stories about what your Dad used to be like, I'm quite glad it's her that you take after."

"Oi!" said Dad walking into the room. "Maybe Molly will take after me ... now that's a scary thought!"

Chapter 11

GOING HOME

"Thank you for coming," Grandma said, giving Archie a kiss on the cheek. Archie wiped it off secretly when she'd turned away.

"Thank you for having them," Mum said for the fifth time. "I won't say that I hope they've not been any trouble, because from all the stories you've told me it's obvious they have!"

"They've been brilliant!" Grandad assured her. "And anyway, you can't complain because they take after you!"

Mum rolled her eyes.

"If they start trying to use your stories as an excuse for bad behaviour …" she began crossly.

"We won't," Archie and Molly sang together, nodding their heads and mouthing "We will" when Mum turned away.

Grandad saw them and smiled.

"Don't go getting me into trouble," he whispered, walking towards the gate and leaning back on it.

"You can do that well enough for yourself …" Mum began. She was interrupted by a loud crack followed by a slow, painful creak as the gate toppled over with Grandad landing on top of it like a domino.

Grandma broke the silence with an unexpected comment.

"Archie," she whispered, "go and peep up the road and check that Mrs Pilkington isn't coming."

Archie!—Look Out

Archie tiptoed carefully past the car and popped his head round the hedge, looking in both directions up and down the street. There was no one there!

"All clear," he whispered, helping Grandad to his feet.

"I've asked you to mend that gate for twenty years!" complained Grandma.

Grandad looked guilty.

"Looks like I know what I'm doing this afternoon," he said, pulling a face at Archie.

Archie was about to climb into the car when the phone rang inside the house.

"Will you just see who that is?" Grandma asked. "You can run quicker than me."

Archie was about to point out that she'd outrun him in the park but decided he didn't really want to tell Mum and Dad about that embarrassing moment, so he ran inside quickly.

He came out wearing an odd expression.

"It was Mrs Pilkington," he said. "She got home last night, took off her hat and my cockroach fell on her knee!"

"Archie!" gasped Mum. "What on earth did you bring that for?"

"Because you said I couldn't bring Terry the tarantula!" Archie replied. "It would have been OK if I had. Mrs Pilkington says she's not scared of spiders but hates cockroaches! And anyway, Terry would have been too big to fire off the sun lounger, so he never would have landed in her hat!"

"I think we'd better go home," Dad suggested, sensing that Mum was getting cross.

"It's OK," Archie added. "I've given her our address, so she's going to post it. She said her husband Fred used to collect realistic plastic insects when he was little, and she found the collection the other day in the wardrobe. And guess what? She's sending them all to me! How about that!"

"Oh no!" Mum groaned, climbing into the car.

"Got quite a friend there!" said Grandad, giving Archie the thumbs up sign.

Archie and Molly climbed into the backseat.

"Look after Goldie!" Molly shouted. "She still looks a bit slow!"

"Come again soon," said Grandma, blowing them a kiss.

"Don't worry," shouted Archie and Molly together. "Nothing would keep us away!"

Dad put the car into gear and set off.

"Stop!" screeched Grandad.

Dad braked.

"OUCH!" shouted Archie. "Molly, why did you pile all those things on the back shelf again?"

Grandad disappeared inside and reappeared waving something in a plastic bag.

"Thought you might like this," he said, giving Archie a wink. "I'll get a new one for me!"

Archie!—Look Out

Archie peeped in the bag and grinned.

"Thaaaaaaaaaaaaaannnnnnnnkkkkkkkkkkkk yooooooooouuuuuuuuuuuuu!" he said, looking at the machine. "Make sure you train the new one before you send an email!"

Dad set off for the second time.

Archie leaned out of the window.

"Byyyyyyyyeeeeeeee!" he shouted.

"OUCH ... Molly, I think I've just been given a matching bruise!"

Chapter 12

LONG JOURNEY!

"**B**oring, boring, boring, boring …" Archie chanted as he gazed out of the car window at the massive traffic jam ahead.

Molly stared at him and lifted her eyebrows in an annoying way.

"Mum says that the word 'bored' is banned in our house," she announced in her most irritating voice. "She says it's 'better to be busy than bored.'"

Archie rolled his eyes and pulled a face, wondering why little sisters always thought they were right, even when it was totally obvious that older brothers knew far more than they did!

"Well, first …" he said cockily, trying to sound intelligent, "…we are not in our house … in case you hadn't noticed, we are in a car! Secondly, if you'd listened properly you'd have realised that I didn't actually say 'bored', I said 'boring'. It's got a different suffix, but I bet you don't know what that means because you're …"

"Archie," interrupted Mum crossly, "stop trying to be clever. Molly isn't as old as you."

Archie sighed loudly.

"Parents are so confusing!" he muttered. "One minute they're telling you to work hard at school and become clever and the next they tell you off for saying clever things!"

"We shouldn't be long now," said Mum, trying to keep the peace.

"You said that two hours ago," grumbled Archie, "and we've only moved about a metre."

"There's obviously been an accident somewhere," said Dad. "We've just got to be patient and be grateful that it's not us."

"I need the toilet," Molly groaned.

"Sorry, love, but you'll have to wait," said Mum.

"But I've been waiting for ages," Molly continued.

"Water, fountain, sea, lake, river, tap, splish, splash, splosh ..." Archie sang.

"Archie!" Mum warned. "Stop it!"

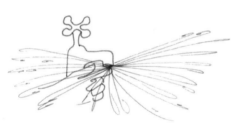

"Drip, drip, splash ..." Archie mumbled softly, leaning close to Molly so Mum couldn't hear. "Oh dear, is it raining? Do you want a drink? Is that a huge waterfall I can hear?"

"Looks like the person in front's having a bit of a problem," said Dad, trying to change the subject by pointing to a thin stream of smoke rising from the bonnet of the car ahead. "I think they'll need to pull over."

Sure enough, the car quickly pulled onto the hard shoulder, and Dad inched forwards until the cars were side by side.

"We've moved three meters!" Archie shouted gleefully, punching the air with his fist and narrowly missing Molly.

"Do you think we should stop?"
Dad asked, looking at the thick black
smoke that was now billowing out
from beneath the bonnet.

"Oh Dad! You can't be serious,"
Archie groaned. "Why do we always
have to stop for everyone?"

"Because we care about people,"
Dad replied, glancing at Mum to see
what she thought.

"But last time you stopped to help
that lady who got a flat tyre you
ended up getting a parking ticket for
stopping on double yellow lines!"
Archie pointed out. "You said it cost
you a fortune!"

"And when Grandma broke down
and you went to help her you got a speeding ticket on the way,"
added Molly. "You said that cost you a fortune too!"

"And that time you tried to help a man who dropped all his
shopping on the floor at the supermarket, someone nicked your
mobile phone out of your pocket while you were picking things
up!" added Archie. "It doesn't exactly make it seem worth
helping!"

"Archie!" warned Mum again. "Even if things go wrong we
should never stop helping other people. It's called 'going the
extra mile.'"

"Well, there's no chance of that here," Archie grumbled. "Going an extra centimetre's impossible in this queue!"

Archie and Molly looked at the man sitting in the driver's seat of the smoking car and then turned to give each other a look which said, "We know what's going to happen next."

"He's very old," Molly whispered, as Dad pulled onto the hard shoulder in front of the car. "He looks about 500!"

"Almost as old as Methuselah," Archie whispered back.

"Methus—a who?" asked Molly, looking confused.

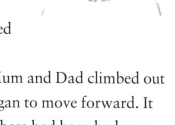

"Oh, someone Johnny told us about who lived for 969 years in the Bible …" Archie explained, "… we'll be at least that old by the time Dad's finished sorting this one out."

At almost the same moment that Mum and Dad climbed out of the car, all the surrounding cars began to move forward. It was obvious that whatever blockage there had been had now been cleared.

"Typical!" Archie muttered, rolling his eyes round and round until he felt slightly dizzy.

After a few moments Dad appeared back at the car and leaned in at the window.

"Can you get my mobile out of my coat pocket, Archie?" he asked. "The man's forgotten his phone, but his family have a farm nearby and we're going to give them a ring. He's quite shaky and so grateful that we stopped. He said he didn't know what he would have done if we'd just driven by."

Archie passed the phone feeling both guilty and cross at the same time.

"We're like the Good Samaritan," Molly announced. "We didn't walk past but instead we stopped!"

"If we'd been walking we'd have been miles away by now," Archie continued to grumble. "In fact, if we'd walked we'd already be at home! Anyway, I just hope that we don't have to take the man to a hotel and spend all our money sorting him out like the Good Samaritan did!"

"It would be quite funny if it cost Dad lots of money for being kind again!" Molly giggled.

Archie saw the funny side and laughed too as Dad appeared again, the old man following behind him.

"You're gong to have to squash up a bit," he said. "Mum's climbing in the back with you, and we're giving Joshua here a lift to his son's house. It's only about two miles away. Another of his children is going to come with the tractor and tow the car back to the farm."

Archie undid his seat belt and moved next to Molly, while Mum crammed in beside him.

Within a few minutes of Joshua climbing into the car, Archie felt glad they'd stopped to help. It turned out that Joshua was sixty-five years old and had five children and twelve grandchildren. He had been a sheep farmer all his life and lived with his wife in a small bungalow on the family farm. Whilst he still liked to help with the animals, two of his children now ran the farm, and they were very busy at the moment as it was the middle of the lambing season.

After five minutes Dad turned off the main road and up a narrow driveway with a signpost at the end of it advertising 'Holly Farm. Bed and Breakfast.' The drive continued for about half a mile before opening into a large farmyard. A man and lady and two children about the same ages as Archie and Molly were waiting for them.

The man shook hands with Dad.

"We can't thank you enough," he said gratefully. "No idea what Dad would have done if you'd not stopped. We're always telling him to take his mobile! Anyway, after this maybe he'll learn! I'm Dave, and this is Grace and our two children Abi and Owen. Come on in, the kettle's on."

Archie and Molly followed the trail of people into the kitchen where an older lady was placing an enormous pile of cakes in the middle of the table! Archie's eyes nearly popped out of his head.

"We've been married over forty years!" the older lady began, nodding towards Joshua. "And he still takes no notice of me when I say 'take your phone'! Anyway, I'm Naomi, and you've come on a good day! Suddenly decided this morning that I felt like baking! Dive in!"

Archie had never really understood the saying 'dive in' when it referred to food. His Mum said it sometimes, and he'd often wondered what she would do if he actually did dive head first into the food she'd made. He decided that now was not a good time to find out! He chose the biggest cake on the plate and was just cramming it into his mouth when he realised Naomi was looking at him in a rather strange way.

He could have understood it if she'd been staring at Molly since her bruise was clearly sticking out underneath her fringe, but he wasn't sure what was wrong with his face.

"You look very familiar to me!" Naomi said suddenly. "You look just like one of our friends …"

"… only a much younger version!" Joshua finished off.

"You don't know Harry and Isabel …"

Naomi was interrupted by Molly shouting, "I think I do!" at the top of her voice and by Archie who, in his eagerness to speak, forgot that his mouth was crammed full of cake and spurted flying crumbs in all directions!

"I don't believe it," said Mum loudly, trying to take the attention away from Archie. "Surely you're not the friends Grandma and Grandad told us about … the ones who got that email?"

Joshua and Naomi nodded, and the rest of the family giggled.

"We hadn't laughed so much in ages," said Naomi, even now wiping a tear from her eye at the thought.

"I laughed more when your Grandad rang to apologise!" chortled Joshua. "I could hear Isabel in the background telling him exactly what to say! Just like Naomi would have done if it had been me!"

"It's a small world," said Dad. "I'm glad we stopped!"

Chapter 13

ON THE FARM

Once Archie had finished making everyone laugh by showing his photographs of their time at Grandad's whilst at the same time sampling every type of cake on the plate, Dave suggested that he take the children to look at some of the newborn lambs. They wandered through the fields, checking on the sheep who were due to give birth to their babies in the next few days and then looked into a barn that was divided up into small pens. Dave explained that often lambs were born out in the fields, but sometimes the sheep were brought inside to give birth so that he could keep a special eye on them. He explained that if the newborn lambs had a bit of difficulty getting used to drinking milk from their mother, they were kept in a pen so that he could help them more easily. In most of the pens the little lambs lay cuddled up to their mothers, but in a few pens tiny lambs were lying in the straw on their own.

"Why are they on their own?" Molly asked. "They look lonely."

"Do you want to hold one?" Dave asked, reaching over the gate and lifting a tiny lamb out of the pen.

Molly looked a bit frightened, but Archie nodded keenly.

"Come and sit here," Dave said, pointing to a bale of straw

on the floor. Archie sat down, and Dave placed the tiny lamb on his knee.

"Sometimes," he explained, "a ewe gets ill and can't feed the lamb. I was walking in the field two nights ago, and I saw a ewe that had obviously just had her lamb, but she was sick. I wasn't sure that the lamb would be alive, but I looked everywhere and eventually found him under a hedge. He was very weak, so I

picked him up and brought him home. We warmed him up by the fire and gave him warm milk out of a bottle, and by the morning he was much stronger. He'll have to stay here for a while, but we're sure he's going to be OK now."

"Do you still feed him out of a bottle?" Molly asked.

"Yes, we'll have to for a few weeks," explained Dave, "just until he can eat proper food. Do you want to have a go?"

By the time Archie and Molly burst back into the kitchen, they were talking non-stop, the boredom of the car journey long forgotten!

"I've held one of the baby lambs!"

"I've fed one of the lambs with a bottle!"

"We've been for a ride on the tractor!"

"I'm starving! Please can I have another cake?"

"I hardly dare say that we need to get back in the car and go home," said Mum, once she could make herself heard above the excitement.

"Oh Mum!" said the children in unison.

Grace opened her mouth to speak, and then thought better of it.

"Can I have a word in private?" she asked, beckoning Mum into the hallway.

A few minutes later, Mum reappeared and whispered something in Dad's ear. He smiled and went outside. Archie could see him speaking to someone on the phone. A few minutes later, he came inside and nodded to Mum.

"What are you whispering about?" Archie asked suspiciously. "You always say it's rude to whisper in public and to go on your phone at someone else's house!"

"Well, I think you'll forgive us when you hear this," Dad replied, a big grin appearing on his face.

"Apparently, Dave and Grace have a family room for four people free for the next two nights, so they wondered if we'd like to stay. We've all got clothes in the car, so we think it's a good idea. Dave says you could go out lambing with him this evening if you wanted …"

"… and we can show you our den!" shouted Abi and Owen together, making everybody jump.

"Our way of saying thank you for rescuing Dad!" Dave added.

As the four children headed towards the door, Dad caught Archie's eye.

"Helping worked this time!" Dad mouthed to him, smiling as Archie nodded and disappeared from view.

Chapter 14

THE RESCUE!

The two days and nights at the farm sped by too quickly, and everyone felt sad to leave, although, to Archie and Molly's delight, before they left Dad booked for them to return to Holly Farm on their next school holidays.

Mum had insisted that they had to arrive home in time for some kind of important committee meeting in the lounge. So Molly had begun watching a film in the kitchen and, to his own surprise, Archie had gone straight up to his bedroom, connected Grandad's microphone to the laptop and begun to finish 'writing' the rest of his diary whilst the visitors arrived downstairs.

"Don't you dare tell anyone that this is the first thing I did when I got in," he ordered Terry, pinging the tarantula up and down on his elastic with the aim of hitting a specific mark on the ceiling. "I might as well finish the diary now I've started it!"

Friday, 5:50pm—Archie's holiday diary:
What a few days! What seemed like a complete disaster of a journey because we were stuck in traffic turned out brillllliiiaannntttlllyyyy! Oh I do like doing thaaaaaaaaaaaat ttttttttt!!!!!!!!! It was funny meeting Grandma and Grandad's friends and eating lots of cake, but the best bit was going out with Dave in the dark looking for lambs. Just me and him and

Abi. We found another little lamb whose mother couldn't feed it—we had to look for ages! It was funny watching Dave. He had great big muscles, and earlier on I'd seen him throwing big bales of hay around, and when I tried to pick them up they were really heavy and I could hardly move them! But when he picked up the little lamb, he was so gentle. He carried it home, wrapped it in a blanket by the fire and we fed it milk off a spoon for while and then out of a bottle later. I watched Dave's face as the lamb got stronger and began to suck. He looked soooooooo happy. Mum doesn't know this, but I sneaked into her room and found a story in the Bible that Johnny told us in Sunday School about a shepherd looking everywhere for a sheep that was lost, even though he already had 99 very healthy ones.

I've heard the story quite a few times before, but now I'd seen Dave's face I wanted to read it again. I think it's hard to believe that God can care for us soooooooooo much that he searches for us and looks soooooooo happy when He finds us!

Anyway, we're going back in the holidays … yiiiippeeee!!!! I think Molly thinks her favourite lamb (Lazarus, she called it) will still be the same size! Mum banned me from saying anything about lamb burgers! She's going to have a chat with Molly sometime!

Anyway, I have to admit I'm glad now that we stopped

Archie!—Look Out

for Joshua's car! It didn't cost Dad any money this time 'cos Dave and Grace wouldn't let them pay for the bed and yummy breakfast because we'd helped their Dad. Maybe helping's not such a bad idea after all.

Oh, that's someone knocking on the door. I thought all Mum's visitors had arrived ... better go and see who it is.

Archie jumped up and looked out of his window. One of the boys from next door was standing below holding a huge box in his hands.

"I'll be down in a minute!" Archie shouted loudly, nearly making the boy jump out of his skin!

He raced downstairs and threw open the door.

"Wow!" he gasped, reading the label. "'Mr Archibald Edwards.' It's for me!"

He carried the parcel carefully into the kitchen and placed it on the table.

"Who's that from?" Molly asked, jumping up to have look.

Archie turned the parcel over carefully. The sender's details were written in small letters in one corner with, to Archie's delight, the shape of a large spider drawn around them.

"It's Mrs Pilkington!" Archie said excitedly. "I didn't expect the box to be so big! It's massive, but it's got to be the insects 'cos Mrs Pilkington's put a spider clue on the back."

"I hope it's not!" muttered Molly. "Just Terry and your cockroach have got you into enough trouble. I dread to think what you could do with a whole boxful!"

Archie grabbed the end of the sticky tape, ripped it off and opened the box. There grinning up at him was Cocky the cockroach.

"Welcome home, Cocky!" announced Archie, lifting him out and pulling back the layers of tissue paper.

"WOOOOOOWWWW!!!"

The box was crammed full of what Archie thought must be the biggest and best and most amazing collection of plastic insects in the whole wide world.

"Mum!" he screamed, completely forgetting that there was a meeting taking place in the lounge.

"Mum!"

Archie grabbed the box and hurtled through the lounge door.

"Mum!"

"Archie! LOOK OUT!" Mum shrieked at the top of her voice.

It was too late. Archie tripped over a handbag (which he would later point out was in a ridiculous position on the floor), and the insects swarmed out of the box, flying in all directions as if they were truly alive. Everyone screamed, and Archie discovered that 'diving' headfirst into food was not a very pleasant experience after all. As he peered out from his chocolate-cake-covered face, he surveyed the damage. A flying cockroach was perched neatly in Mrs Wiggleworth's hair; two stick insects were disguised as part of a straw hat lying on the arm of a chair; what looked like Terry's twin was clinging to the arm of a lady who seemed to have frozen as she lifted her drink to her mouth; millipedes, centipedes, a variety of mites, locusts, crickets and beetles of every kind scattered the carpet, and a huge emperor scorpion was seated on top of Mum's head.

Friday, 6.10pm—Archie's holiday diary:
I am banished to my bedroom until the visitors go! Not really a punishment 'cos I am happy to be here with my insects forever! Mum will laugh later when she sees the funny side of all of this! ... I think!
Just me and about 5 million insects. Terry and Cocky have never looked so happy. Oh, the fun we will have. And the best bit is I've finished my diary! I've done my homework! SO now I can just play ... play ... play for the rest of the holiday!
Yiiippppeeeeee!!!

Also available

ARCHIE! TV STAR

Rebecca Parkinson

'TV star' is the comical story of a boy called Archie who always seems to get into trouble, especially from the ferocious head teacher, Mrs Dimple. He loves football, hates school, has an interesting collection of friends, is dreading the move into Year 4 after the summer holidays and can't quite understand how the stories in the Bible fit in with his life today!

However, for Archie surprises are afoot and the autumn term sees him not only beginning to enjoy the year, but also visiting a TV studio to star in the school Christmas play! However, things are never straight forward and allergic reactions, unusual television presenters, tarantulas and other traumas lead to a hilarious and sometimes moving story.

The book follows Archie through the highs and lows of school life as he and his friends learn that God loves them just the way they are.

Rebecca Parkinson lives in Lancashire with her husband and their two children. As a teacher and the leader of the youth and children's team in her church, she loves to pass the Bible stories on to others in a way that everyone can understand.

Also available

RICHES IN ROMANIA

Rebecca Parkinson

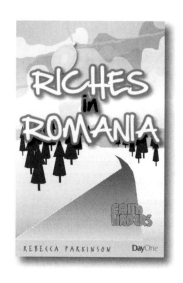

Jenny's parents have always been able to give her everything she wants until her dad begins a new job working for a Christian charity. As Jenny struggles to come to terms with their new lifestyle, her family is invited to take part in a farming project in Romania and Jenny sets off on an adventure that will ultimately change her life!

As Jenny and her brother David spend time in a small Romanian village, they make friends with the local children and begin to realise that friendship can break down barriers of wealth, language and culture. However, when Jenny's precious locket goes missing it seems that everything has gone wrong, until a guard, previously in the Communist regime, teaches her the secret of forgiveness and encourages her to set about putting things right in her own life.

It is hoped that this book will introduce children to life in Romania. It aims to show how many of us have become so caught up in materialism that we have lost something of the purpose and the wonder of life. It also aims to show how the love of God breaks down barriers and that forgiveness is the only way to live happy and fulfilled lives.

Seed Picture Making

Seed Picture Making

by
Roger and Glenda Marsh

London
Blandford Press

First published 1973
by Blandford Press Ltd,
167 High Holborn, London WC1V 6PH

© 1973 Roger and Glenda Marsh

ISBN 0 7137 0625 2

Text set in 12 on 13 Bembo and
printed in Great Britain by
Unwin Brothers Limited
Old Woking, Surrey
A Member of the Staples Printing Group

List of Contents

Acknowledgements

It is with pleasure that we place on record our appreciation for the help and advice given to us by John E. Haith Ltd, of Cleethorpes, Lincolnshire.

We would also like to thank those students who gave us permission to reproduce their work.

R. and G. M.

I would like to make a personal acknowledgement in gratitude to the late Mrs Struan Sorren who initially introduced me to this medium over a decade ago.

G. M.

There is nothing quite like seeds, each one a miracle of nature, a product of the earth. They have been used from time immemorial for sowing, cooking, grinding and baking; and, which may be more surprising, for ornamentation and adornment, for minute formers in tie and dye fabric work and to produce graphic images. The craft of working with seeds as an artistic medium is not new.

Working with seeds will open up to those people not conversant with this medium a whole new spectrum of activity, for one is forced, when choosing particular seeds for a particular subject idea, to abandon one's pre-conceptions of colour, texture and form and, in a sense, while still keeping the original picture in mind, to let the seeds dictate its development.

The mechanics of seed-laying are very basic. The principle of attaching seeds to a firm base by means of a clear-drying glue is a simple enough procedure and anyone prepared to spend a little time and to take a little care may try their hand and be successful. Of course, the work has to be executed with forethought and planning, not haphazardly or by guess-work. The aim of this book is to set before the reader various techniques and helpful information for every stage in seed picture making which we have learned over many years. We hope that an understanding of the textural and design properties of seeds will lead the reader to produce finished work of very high quality.

All the seeds mentioned in this book are non-poisonous, but there is a danger that seeds collected or purchased abroad in the form of necklaces will be toxic. It is safe to assume that seeds intended for consumption by birds or by humans, seeds from vegetables, flowers and fruit, are not poisonous, but outside of this list we do advise you to be cautious and to check up on the seed properties to eliminate the danger to your health.

1 Materials and equipment

To make a seed picture you will require a baseboard, seeds, glue and various other materials for applying the seeds and varnishing the picture.

The baseboard

As the name suggests, this is the base on which the seeds will be attached. The baseboard should be perfectly flat and rigid, preferably lightweight and with a matt surface. Materials most suitable for this purpose are hardboard, 6mm. plywood or thick cardboard (e.g. mounting board).

The seeds
(*See* classification table, pp. 12–19).

The two main sources of suitable seeds are a bird seed merchant and a local grocery or supermarket. Flower and vegetable packet seeds may also be obtained from a garden centre and, of course, you can always extract and preserve the seeds of fruit, flowers and vegetables yourself (*see* p. 20).

Bird seed merchants generally carry stock seeds such as sunflower, maize, millet, hemp, linseed, peas and mixed varieties.

Local groceries and supermarkets, etc. stock rice, split peas, lentils, pearl barley, and so on.

Garden pack seeds. Seeds within this category have yet to be fully investigated as picture-making material, but the variety of shapes, sizes and textures offer interesting possibilities. Unfortunately, the price of a packet can make the use of these seeds very expensive.

Other materials

Seed containers

With the quantity and variety of seeds that you will probably want to use, it will be necessary to find a method of storage. Almost any cardboard box or tin with a lid will suffice; we have found herb drums ideal. Providing that the containers are durable, they should provide satisfactory storage. A label attached to each container marking its contents will avoid any confusion and provide a quick and easy identification.

Seed dispenser

The application of the smaller seeds to the design can present a problem, and a seed dispenser will prove invaluable. This can take many different forms, providing that it can hold a quantity of seeds, while releasing the required number for the design.

An old icing set is ideal for this purpose. The interchangeable nozzles are most suitable for dealing with the varying seed sizes. Other items found useful are salt and pepper pots, and empty containers which had a previous dispensing function, such as saccharin tablet dispensers.

Tweezers

Tweezers are a useful aid to placing the larger seeds accurately on to the glued areas of the design. Ordinary household tweezers will suffice.

Glue

Glues that are intended to stick wood or plastic have been found to be the most suitable for seed work, but there are many other all purpose glues which can be used provided that they are clear-drying, harden within a matter of hours and are of the 'cement' and not 'impact' type. 'Evostick ResinW', 'Dufix' 'UHU',

9

'Bostick 1' and 'Copydex' are all glues which we have found particularly suitable.

Spatula

A plastic spatula for spreading the glue is most useful. Sometimes a spatula or spreader is provided with the glue, or built into the cap of the tube.

Guiding stick

This item is for moving, prodding and settling the seeds into their positions. The guide stick can take almost any form, providing it is able to do the job— an empty ballpoint pen, a lollipop stick or even a pencil!

Kraft knife

A kraft knife is ideal for splitting the larger seeds and cutting card. It is far safer and more stable than a razor blade.

Polyurethane varnish (see p. 57)

This is used when the seed picture has been completed. A thin coat is brushed gently over the entire picture area, to give it a protective film, and aid seed bonding. It also has the effect of bringing up the colour of the seeds, and imparting a glossy finish. Polyurethane varnish can be purchased in tins containing a quarter of a pint (142 ml) upwards. There are also clear spray varnishes which may be used. These, however, require several thin coats to achieve the desired effect. The following have been used successfully: 'Ronseal', 'Translac Permshine' clear sealers; and 'U Spray' clear varnish.

Brushes for varnishing

A 2–in. (5–cm.) household painting brush will do the job satisfactorily.

Solvent

The brush should be cleaned immediately in the solvent recommended by the manufacturer of the varnish, usually white spirit.

The following classification table of seeds is far from exhaustive, but it does contain those seeds which are readily available in most parts of the country. This range can be extended considerably by private investigation into both regular and less conventional sources. It is hoped that this table will provide you with a source of reference for the identification and uses of the various seeds which you are likely to need when making seed pictures.

The list is in alphabetical order for easy consultation, and no attempt has been made to group the seeds according to colour, size or botanical family. The final column, source of supply, is coded with the initials of where the seeds may be obtained. The seeds have been drawn actual size beside their descriptions on alternating sides of the table.

B.S.M.—bird seed merchant (mainly pet shops).
G & S—grocery and supermarket.
G.S.   —gardening shop.
D   —delicatessen.
H.P.   —home preservation.

2 Choosing your seeds—a classification table

Key

Fig. 2 A haphazard arrangement of many of the different types of seeds mentioned in the seed classification table overleaf. It may be of interest to the reader to know that some of these seeds were painted silver. This is allowable, but only just!

Name	Description
Apple pip	Tear-shaped. Brown, ranging from light to dark. Glossy.
Beetroot	Crumpled form similar to a screwed-up piece of paper. Buff. Matt.
Black eye beans	Kidney-shaped. Cream with a black 'eye' surrounding the white hilum. Matt, crepe-like surface.
Black pepper corn	Spherical. Dark brown. Heavily wrinkled surface.
Black rape	Spherical. Black. Matt surface.
Buckwheat	Three-sided. Ends pointed. Dark tan. Slightly glossy.
Butter beans	Kidney-shaped. Large and flat. Cream. Matt.
Caraway seeds	Curved tiny banana shape. Five-'sided'. Brown with cream stripes dividing the surface sections. Matt.
Cherry	Oval shape with a dividing seam all round. Pinky cream. Matt.
Chick pea	Lumpy spherical shape. Warm beige. Semi-matt.
Chicory	Tiny cone shape. Varying from light fawn to dark brown. Matt.
Clipped oats	Torpedo shape. Pale gold.
Coffee beans. Unroasted	Two forms: (a) large, flat on one side, domed on other, (b) smaller, tightly curved. Seam on under side. Colour: Uganda—marbled pale green, Costa Rica —darker green, Kenya—mid green. Matt.
Coffee beans. Roasted	Same shape as above. Colour varies depending on the roast from warm light brown to rich dark brown.

Other Information	Source
Apples should be mature or the seeds will be white and soft.	H.P.
A fascinating crinkly texture can be achieved with this.	G.S. H.P.
Natural laying position places the eye on the side. In order to gain the best effect the bean must be attached by the spine.	D
Generally used in small quantities. Price would be prohibitive for large amounts.	G & S
Useful for detail and can be laid as background colour, although can be difficult to control in quantity. Comes mainly from Holland. Used instead of mustard in mustard and cress as it is superior.	B.S.M.
Its three sides make it easy to lay, yet interesting as each seed appears to have a spine. Grown in England, South Africa, Australia.	B.S.M.
Fills large areas quickly. Subject to discoloration when varnished.	G & S
Useful for detail and for laying as a background. Gives an interesting surface texture. (Smell pleasant!)	G & S
A relief seed. Too hard to split.	H.P.
Its irregular form offers an interesting relief texture.	D
Useful as a variegated background colour. Come from France, Italy.	B.S.M.
Unsuitable for fine detail. Valuable for pattern, texture and linear statements.	B.S.M.
This bean is grown in two forms which are mixed to improve the flavour. The colour varies according to the country of origin. Can be attached seam up or down.	D
Gives a rich, satisfying dark brown tone with a pleasant humped surface. Easier to lay flat side down.	G & S

Name	Description
Cyprus tares	Slightly flattened sphere shape. Varying from khaki, through speckled browns to slate grey. Semi-matt.
Dill	Flat oval shape. Brown surrounded with a fawn rim. Matt.
Dutch blue maw	Minute kidney shape. Predominantly blue-grey. Matt.
Dwarf french bean	Elongated kidney shape. Varying from light to dark crimson with gold markings. Glossy.
English wildseed	Too varied to describe but generally small. Mixed fawns and golds. Matt.
Groats	Cylindrical. Pale gold. Matt.
Golden pleasure (Gold of pleasure)	Minute oval shape. Hot ginger red. Matt.
Gunger peas	Flattened sphere with a hilum on one straight edge. Mushroom-coloured seed with speckles and patches of chestnut. Some are totally grey or completely chestnut.
Haricot beans	Rounded oval shape. Greenish white. Glossy.
Hemp	Rounded oval with a seam round. Greenish grey. Glossy.
Honesty	Shaped like a waterlily leaf. Dark brown with darker veins. Matt.
Iris (bearded)	Oval. Pointed at one end. Pale gold. Matt.
Iris (yellow flag)	Cylindrical section. Flat on each side. Pale fawn. Semi-matt.
Jack millet	Spherical middle, pointed at each end. Fawn with husk. Ochre with husk removed. Glossy when husked.
Kidney beans	Large kidney shape. Rosy purple with black speckles spreading out from the hilum. Glossy.
Linseed	Flattened leaf shape. Rich tan. Glossy.

Other Information	*Source*
Have the appearance of smooth river pebbles. It is recommended that they are sorted into their various colours.	B.S.M.
Useful for background. (Smell pleasant!)	D
Too small for anything except using in quantity. Come from poppies. Nearest seed to blue colouring.	B.S.M.
Attractive pattern and rich colour. A relief seed.	G.S.
These are mostly grass seeds. Impossible to sort. Useful for texture.	B.S.M.
These are oats which have been husked.	B.S.M.
Use in quantity. Too small to handle individually. Known to have been used commercially for the seeds in 'raspberry' jam. Provides a rarely seen rich red.	B.S.M.
These seeds are eye catching in their random colour variation. It is worth sorting out the plain ones also for use as a solid colour.	D
A relief seed. Easy to handle. Subject to discoloration when varnished.	G & S
Imported from Manchuria and Chile. Useful for bubbly texture.	B.S.M.
Very easy to fix as they are flat and of a convenient size. Excellent covering properties.	H.P.
Similar to a small pea. Useful for defining contour and also filling large areas.	H.P.
Easy to fix. Useful for outline.	H.P.
Rather small for using individually. Useful as a dark flesh tone. Of a handy size for detailed pictures.	B.S.M.
Richly coloured and patterned seed. Ideal for large areas. Strong relief seed.	G.S.
Useful in a detailed picture. Rich colour. Grown in England and Holland from the flax plant.	B.S.M.

15

Name	Description
Lupin	Oval with a hilum on short edge. Dark khaki to brown. Glossy.
Maize	Tear-shaped, flat on two sides. Varies from pale orange to red, lighter at the thin end. Glossy.
Maple peas	Spherical. Varying from gold-speckled pale green to ginger-speckled gold. Semi-glossy.
Marigold	Hook shape with a spiky spine on outer edge. Buff colour. Matt.
Marrow	Tear drop shape. Flat with a distinct rim around the edge. Cream. Matt.
Mazagan canary	Wheat-shaped. Golden. Very glossy.
Melon	Flat oval with a seam all round. Creamy white. Matt.
Milo	Flattened sphere shape. Ranging in colour from red speckled gold to golden brown. Matt.
Niger	Thin, splinter-shaped. Black. Glossy.
Orange pip	A round seed encased in a woody coat pointed at each end. Cream. Matt.
Paddy rice	Oval. Pointed at each end. Has a raised central section on each side. Gold. Matt.
Panicum millet	Lemon-shaped. Pale gold. Semi-matt.
Parsley	Similar to caraway seeds but smaller.
Parsnip	Oval. Varying from green to gold with two distinct black stripes. Matt.
Patna rice	Long oval shape. Varying from grey white to fawn depending on variety. Translucent. Matt.

Other Information	Source
Useful in detailed pictures.	H.P.

Comes in several sizes. The smaller is 'popcorn'. The largest type comes from America. A relief seed. Very good for pattern-making.   B.S.M. G & S

A relief seed. Not easy to fix due to spherical nature. If shelled and halved they are yellow. Useful in large patterns and textures.   B.S.M.

A fascinating seed, possibly unique in shape. Excellent for surface interest.   H.P.

A useful covering seed. Easy to lay.   H.P. G.S.

Useful in a detailed picture. Gives a rich glossy sheen in quantity. Comes from Morocco.   B.S.M.

Useful for covering large areas. Dye very easily. Easy to fix.   H.P.

Useful as a flesh tone. An intriguing colour for use in texture and pattern. Comes from Argentina.   B.S.M.

A very useful little seed. The nearest thing to a line. Worth the trouble of handling individually. Interesting as a texture in quantity. Comes from India and Ethiopia.   B.S.M.

Good relief seed. Similar size to haricot bean but more textured.   H.P.

Can be laid individually. Useful for pattern and texture. Comes from Argentina and Far East.   B.S.M.

Useful for flesh tone. Too small for individual use. More useful for colour than for texture.   B.S.M.

Useful for texture.   G.S.

A delicate seed with a slightly embossed appearance.   G.S. H.P.

Can be handled either in a linear fashion or in large areas. Can be laid on a coloured ground allowing this to show dimly through the seeds.   G & S

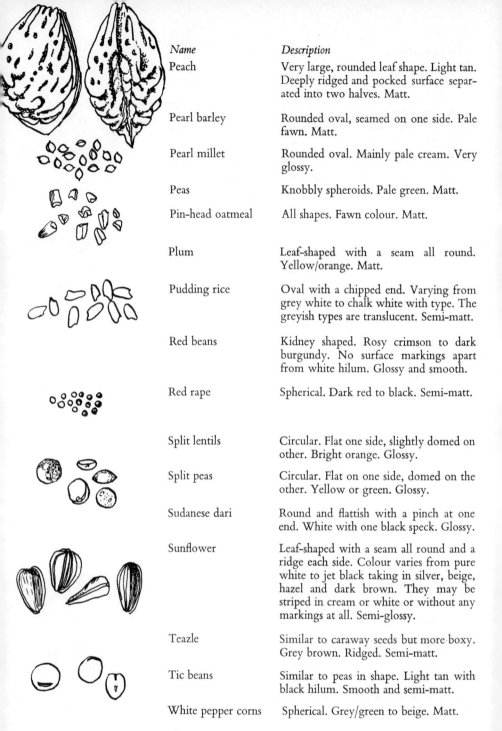

Name	Description
Peach	Very large, rounded leaf shape. Light tan. Deeply ridged and pocked surface separated into two halves. Matt.
Pearl barley	Rounded oval, seamed on one side. Pale fawn. Matt.
Pearl millet	Rounded oval. Mainly pale cream. Very glossy.
Peas	Knobbly spheroids. Pale green. Matt.
Pin-head oatmeal	All shapes. Fawn colour. Matt.
Plum	Leaf-shaped with a seam all round. Yellow/orange. Matt.
Pudding rice	Oval with a chipped end. Varying from grey white to chalk white with type. The greyish types are translucent. Semi-matt.
Red beans	Kidney shaped. Rosy crimson to dark burgundy. No surface markings apart from white hilum. Glossy and smooth.
Red rape	Spherical. Dark red to black. Semi-matt.
Split lentils	Circular. Flat one side, slightly domed on other. Bright orange. Glossy.
Split peas	Circular. Flat on one side, domed on the other. Yellow or green. Glossy.
Sudanese dari	Round and flattish with a pinch at one end. White with one black speck. Glossy.
Sunflower	Leaf-shaped with a seam all round and a ridge each side. Colour varies from pure white to jet black taking in silver, beige, hazel and dark brown. They may be striped in cream or white or without any markings at all. Semi-glossy.
Teazle	Similar to caraway seeds but more boxy. Grey brown. Ridged. Semi-matt.
Tic beans	Similar to peas in shape. Light tan with black hilum. Smooth and semi-matt.
White pepper corns	Spherical. Grey/green to beige. Matt.

Other Information	*Source*
One of the largest seeds. Very interesting texturally. Must be used whole as it is too hard to split. Used in high relief.	H.P.
Can be laid individually. Use for texture or pattern.	B.S.M.
A good size and shape for detail work. Provides shiny highlights.	B.S.M.
Varying in size depending on type. A relief seed.	G & S
This is oatmeal crushed. Provides an interesting random texture.	B.S.M.
A fairly large, relief seed. Difficult to split.	H.P.
All purpose seed for tonal contrast, pattern and outline. Colour variation can be provided with a coloured background.	G & S
Pattern, texture and outline but not for small detail pictures. A relief seed.	D
This is black rape bleached for better selling as a birdseed. Can be laid in either detail or quantity but is somewhat difficult to handle.	B.S.M.
Strong bright colour. Easy to attach.	G & S
All purpose seed. Not for fine detail. Pleasant texture. Easy to attach.	G & S
Its whiteness together with its size makes this seed an excellent all-rounder.	B.S.M.
One of the most versatile and interesting seeds. Comes in many sizes. Can be split readily or used whole in many positions to form varying textures. The stripes can show direction of form. It is excellent due to its colour variation for using tonally. Comes from Kenya and Australia.	B.S.M.
Can be used individually or in quantity for texture. Imported from Italy and France.	B.S.M. H.P.
A relief seed. Spherical shape requires bedding well into glue.	B.S.M.
A relief seed. Texture.	G & S

3 Preservation and preparation

Many seeds are only economical to obtain if one preserves them oneself. Indeed, some seeds (date, plum, peach, etc.) are unobtainable in any other way. Preserving requires a little time and the application of a simple procedure.

Fruit seeds

Fruit seeds, for example, blackberry, raspberry, orange, apple, lemon, melon, date, grape, cherry and even the seeds of more unusual fruits, lichees for instance, should be preserved as the opportunity arises.

Rinse the seeds gently in tepid water to remove any residue of the fruit and stickiness. To dry the seeds, spread them thinly on blotting paper or dry sand in a tray. Newspaper will suffice if blotting paper is not available, and the sand tray can take the form of an old dinner plate or baking tray. Place the seeds in a dark, dry and well-ventilated place, such as a garden shed, pantry or spare room, and allow them to dry naturally, turning them regularly. The above conditions are necessary because sunlight has a tendency to discolour the seeds by bleaching them or turning them yellow. A dry atmosphere is obviously needed to dry the seeds and ventilation prevents the growth of fungus, mould or mildew, which may rot or discolour the seeds. Generally, the larger seeds are placed on the sand tray while those which are too small and less easy to separate from the sand, can be placed on the paper.

Flower seeds

The seeds from nasturtium, marigolds, poppies, lupins or sunflowers can give very interesting qualities to seed pictures. Unlike fruit trees and vegetables, flowers distribute their seeds well before the plant dies down. Therefore, the seed pods or dead flower heads must be gathered before the seeds are dry and mature. They should be tied in bunches and hung upside down in a dry, well-ventilated place, preferably with a muslin bag around the heads to prevent the seeds dropping away and being lost.

Insect pests, such as earwigs, have a tendency to

make their homes in dead flower heads. To prevent unpleasant surprises, therefore, it is a good idea, with plants which are particularly susceptible, to spray them with an insect killer before hanging them up!

Fig. 3 Dead flower heads, collected and ready for drying.

Vegetable seeds

Seeds from vegetables, such as peas, beans of various colours, marrows, onions, tomatoes and sweet corn, offer another source for collection. These seeds can be removed from the plants when they have literally 'gone to seed', to cut down on the length of the drying time. The seeds can be extracted earlier, but they will then have to be dried in the same way as fruit seeds.

Additional sources

There are many other varieties and types of seeds which do not fit into the categories listed above, yet are equally useful, for example, the cereals wheat, barley and oats, and various grasses. These can be dried in the same manner as flowers.

We consider the drying procedure mentioned here to be the most successful, but individuals will probably develop their own methods. The sun, for instance, can help to dry the seeds and providing that the seeds are shielded by a cover, this works quite well. It will be necessary, however, to occupy table-top space for a week or so, and this might prove inconvenient.

Preparing the seeds In the majority of cases seeds that have been pre-served or purchased require very little or no attention before use.

Seeds that have been preserved locally can usually be used immediately they are dry. Those seeds that were 'left on the plant' to dry and mature should be removed from their sockets, cases or pods. After removal it is advisable to clean the seeds by placing them between the folds of a soft cloth and gently rubbing them to remove dust particles, etc.

Shop seeds can also be used straightaway, although the larger seeds may have to be split. This also applies to the large preserved seeds.

Splitting It will be found necessary to split those large seeds that are so rounded in section that they would be awkward to attach to the baseboard. By cutting them in half, a flat plain is achieved, which will allow the seeds to be attached securely, and also prevent them from projecting too far above the height of the other seeds. Seeds that will need to be split include sun-flower, orange, marrow and kidney beans.

To split a seed, place it on a cutting board (a waste piece of cardboard will suffice) and position the blade of the kraft knife along the seam or edge of the seed. Press down carefully and firmly so that the blade cuts through. The seed may be held firm with a pair of tweezers to make the cutting operation safer. Once

split in two, the kernels, which can be easily extracted, should be taken out and discarded.

Fig. 4 Large seeds may be split so that the flat plane can be attached securely to the baseboard.

There are, of course, seeds that are too hard to split with a kraft knife, such as date or cherry seeds, and these can only be prised open with much more pressure than is safe to attempt with a knife. It is better to leave these seeds as they are, unless a safe facility is available to split them.

Colours

One may find among the seeds available a multitude of beautiful colours. It is noticeable, however, that there is a bias towards the yellow/orange end of the spectrum and a distinct gap where the blue/violet section should be. There are many pure and beautiful yellows to be found, for instance in split peas, panicum, oats, and an abundance also of oranges (lentils, maize) and rich browns (linseed, golden pleasure). Niger is, as the name suggests, a very strong black, as is black

23

rape, and as these two seeds are of an entirely different form they are a very useful addition to the 'palette'. Ordinary household rice gives a pure translucent white and again it is available in varying shapes, pudding rice and patna (long grain) rice. Sunflower seeds may also be plain white though of course they are more familiar in their black/grey and white colouring. The striped colouring of the sunflower seed is excellent for patterning large areas quickly, and placed against the background of other seed varieties it is ideal for marking out important features. It shows up particularly well as most seeds are of a solid colour rather than patterned.

In searching for colours outside of the 'autumn' range we experienced some difficulty. Dutch blue maw, despite its name, is not truly a blue colour but more of a slate grey. However, it can be used at a pinch particularly if it is placed in juxtaposition to other very distinct colours when it will show up as blue. We found that the green variety of split pea gives a strong green colour but when exposed to strong light it shows a tendency to turn yellow, which may defeat the colour scheme. Unroasted coffee beans also have pale green shades. A true red is not easily come by either, though many of the rich brown seeds will bridge the gap quite satisfactorily.

Clearly, the range of colours, though biased heavily towards the warm side of the spectrum, is quite wide. Ideally we should utilize the natural warm tones to achieve the characteristic seed mosaic. These natural colours have a charm which synthetic ones can never possess, and one should strive to enhance them by careful organization and usage. One can, however, with a little ingenious colouring of the baseboard, achieve a subtle variation of the colouring. For instance rice, being slightly translucent, readily shows tinges of the colour it is covering. Even if the seeds themself are opaque some of the baseboard colour will usually show between the seeds providing the desired

Fig. 5(a) This illustration was designed to show how colouring the baseboard affects the tone of the seeds. Note that the lentils on the arm and the rice grains around the foot are much lighter than the lentils and rice elsewhere; this was the result of painting the baseboard in a lighter colour at these points.

Fig. 5(b) A close-up of the above showing how a dark background makes the rice grains on the face seem two-toned.

colour. A small experiment may be carried out with baseboard colouring to give one some idea of the possibilities. Taking a strip of card, paint it in bands of varying colours, e.g. try bright colours such as red or purple and more subtle ones such as pink or pale blue. Use poster paint or gouache as these are easily handled and of a good colour strength. Now lay rice closely all along the card and observe the variations in colour and tone. The same experiment may be tried using other opaque seeds.

Dyeing   It may be, however, that one has a special effect in mind for which only very brightly coloured seeds will serve. Seeds themselves sometimes have brilliant colours, but as has been noted they are notably lacking in true blue and bright red. If the lack of these colours presents a problem then the seeds may, as a last resort, be dyed. We do not recommend this procedure from an aesthetic viewpoint as the colours invariably are out of sympathy with the true colours of the seeds. The tendency is for them to look synthetic beside the glowing, natural colours. Not all seeds will accept dye satisfactorily, but those which have been husked, for example rice, and those which have semi-absorbant shells, like melon seeds, take the colour quite well. We have found the most readily available and convenient dye is food colouring, the kind which is used for cake decoration, for instance, cochineal. Ordinary coloured writing or drawing ink will also give a good effect. It is quite simple to place the required amount of seeds into a dish and trickle a little dye colour onto them. They should then be stirred until evenly covered. The strength of colour will depend on how long they are left before drying. They should be dried thoroughly on blotting paper or paper tissues before using in a picture.

Fig. 6 'The owl' (12 in. × 14 in. —30·5 cm. × 35·6 cm) by Finola Coudrey. Rice seeds on the branch were dyed dark brown and rice in the sky was dyed blue.

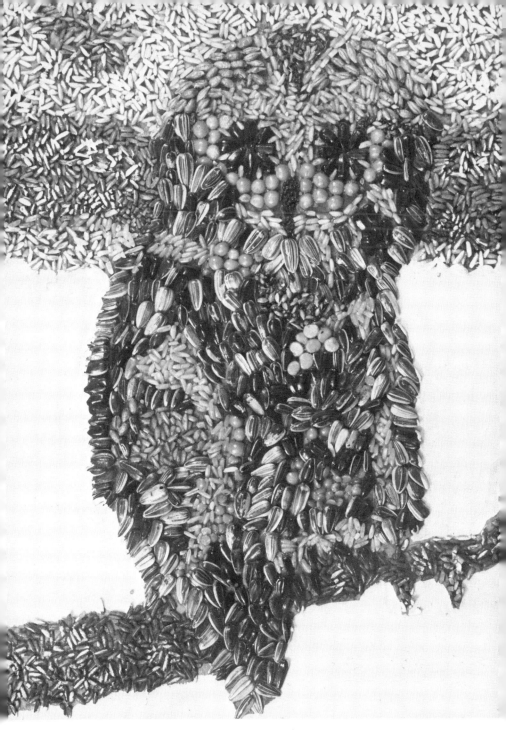

4 Designing the picture

The design for a seed picture should not be produced in isolation from the seeds, but thought of in terms of the seeds. A little experience in handling seeds soon reveals their potential and their limitations and it is these two aspects which most strongly influence the formation of a picture. Other considerations to be borne in mind are the size of the picture, the variety of seeds available and the quantity required. This information, again, can only be gained through working with seeds. Previous experience not only allows the artist to assess size, quantity, etc., but permits him to judge whether his idea for a picture is practical, and not impossible, to carry out. It cannot be over-emphasized that to attempt a full-scale seed picture from a design conceived without any practical knowledge of seeds will, in the majority of cases, court disaster. (*See* 'Experimenting', Chapter 6.)

Subject matter

The choice of subject matter is determined by a number of factors which will differ with each individual: environment, interests, education, influences. It is, therefore, almost impossible to offer specific suggestions, although we have endeavoured to give some imaginative guide lines in Chapter 7, to which reference can be made.

Once the subject matter has been decided upon, the idea has to be translated into visual form by producing a number of preparatory drawings. It is advised that the design should be fully worked out at this stage, and all aspects considered. One should endeavour to work to actual size, but should it be favoured to work smaller, it will be necessary to scale up to the actual size when transferring the design to the baseboard. Finally, before the drawing is transferred, draw a line round it to enclose it.

The baseboard

Before the transfer of the design is discussed, a word about the baseboard upon which the design is to be transferred.

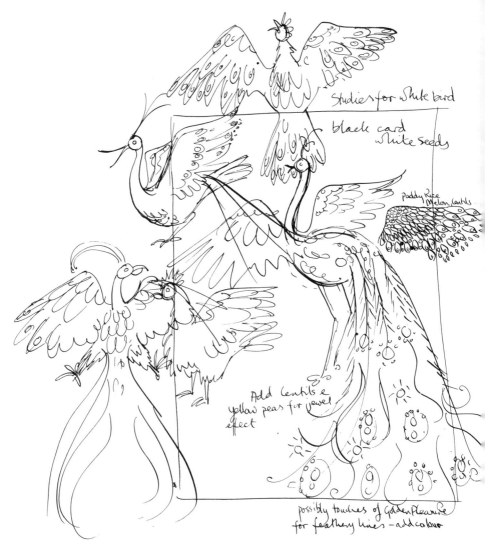

Within the illustration (handwritten annotations):

Studies for White bird

black card
white seeds

Paddy Rice
Melon Lentils

Add Lentils &
yellow peas for jewel
effect

possibly touches of Golden Pheasant
for feathery lines – add colour

The material for the baseboard can be selected from those suggested in Chapter 1. Having decided upon the material, a size should be purchased measuring $\frac{1}{2}$ in. (1·3 cm.) larger than the design ($\frac{1}{4}$ in.—0·6 cm. all round). The colour of the baseboard has to be considered, for the colour has a direct effect upon the overall colour of the picture. For example, rice grains attached to a white ground will appear opaque, whereas the same seeds attached to a dark ground will

Fig. 7 These were the initial drawings for the cover picture, 'Flapping bird'. In this instance they were a sufficient basis on which to begin.

29

Figs. 8(a) and (b) This design was worked out in detail (a) and then transferred on to the baseboard free hand (b). You can see the completed work in Plate 5.

appear in parts to be transluscent (*see* Figs. 5 (a) and (b)). Small areas of a baseboard will almost inevitably be seen between certain varieties of seeds, and this can have the effect of making seeds appear darker or lighter. In some cases, poor colour selection can be obtrusive to the picture. The choice of base colour should be complementary to the general mass of the seeds, and be in harmony. Should the baseboard not be of the colour best suited to the design, it can be painted with household paint. If card is to be used, it can be purchased in a colour or tone nearest to that required.

A further aid to matching the baseboard to the seeds is to paint areas of the baseboard in various tones of colour where seeds of comparative tones will be attached. This practice is to be recommended, but it may be found practicable only with the larger seed masses.

When a suitable ground colour has been laid and has hardened, a light rubbing with sandpaper over the painted area will give a tooth to hold the seeds securely. The baseboard is now ready to accept the design.

The transfer

There are a number of ways in which the design can be transferred on to the baseboard. The simplest and most direct methods are drawing free hand, 'squaring up' or using carbon paper.

Free hand drawing involves transferring the design by eye; this executed successfully can produce a lively design with a spontaneity which can carry through to the final picture.

Squaring up is concerned with gridding both the drawing and the baseboard. The squares on the baseboard will be drawn larger or smaller in relation to those on the drawing depending on whether the finished result is desired to be larger or smaller. Finally, the drawing is transferred from the design by plotting its position from the squares and then redrawing onto the corresponding squares on the base-

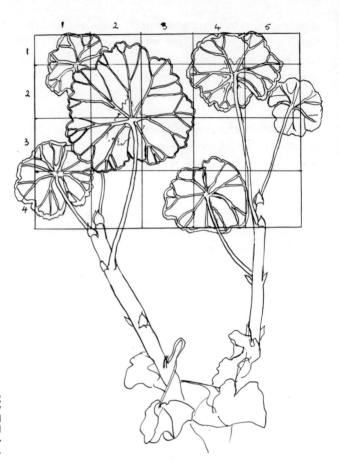

Figs. 9(a) and *opposite* (b) Squaring up. This was the preliminary work for Plate 4. The original design (a) was squared up and then redrawn on the baseboard in larger proportions (b).

board. The size of the squares is governed by the detail contained within the design; the more detail there is the smaller the squares and vice versa.

Dressmaker's *carbon paper* is the simplest method to use, requiring the artist to place a sheet of carbon paper between the baseboard and the design. The carbon, which is in contact with the baseboard, will leave a mark on the baseboard where pressure was applied through the drawing. The carbon paper is manufactured in several colours, which enables the transferred carbon to be seen on a variety of coloured baseboards.

The transferred drawing produced by the first two

Plate I 'Portrait of Roger' (see p. 48)

Plate 2 'Period piece' (see p. 51)

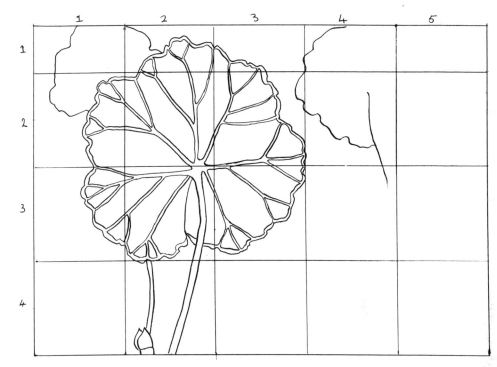

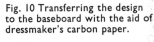

Fig. 9(b)

methods, free hand and squaring up, can be drawn with a pencil, fibre tip pen, ball point pen, or pen and indian ink. A drawing transferred by carbon paper should remain legible until the seed picture is complete, but as a precaution the carbon drawing can be drawn over with indian ink.

Fig. 10 Transferring the design to the baseboard with the aid of dressmaker's carbon paper.

5 Seed-laying

Before beginning to lay the seeds, it is advisable to assemble all the materials and equipment you will need for the picture, and all the seeds you have selected.

Materials

Glue
Tweezers
Seed dispenser
Spatula
Seed guiding stick
Prepared baseboard
Seeds (*see* classification table, pp. 12-19)

Technique

The technique for attaching seeds to the baseboard is reasonably straightforward, providing that a few basic rules are observed, but it is strongly recommended that you try out a few test pieces before starting a full-scale work. This way you will avoid disappointments and wasting materials. The physical act of gluing seeds to a board does require a little organization and careful handling.

Attach the seeds with clear-drying glue, spread liberally but never so that the seeds will sink totally into the glue. Lay only a small area of glue at a time so that it does not harden before you are ready to attach seeds to that area. When the appropriate seeds are firmly bedded, a further film of glue can be extended to the surrounding area and more seeds applied. By working one small section at a time and allowing it to dry, the design can be continued without disturbing the seeds already laid.

Care should be taken not to allow the glue to touch the face of the seeds. If it does squeeze up over the sides, it will spoil the general appearance of the picture.

Procedure

Begin the seed-laying operation with a detailed area, preferably working from the top of the design downwards. When working with detail, it is especially important to lay glue only in the immediate area to

Fig. 11 The handle of a spoon can be employed to settle the newly laid seeds into the glue.

be worked, as seeds often have to be positioned individually and this requires care, patience and a little time. Having completed the first detailed area, the seeds providing the background surrounding it can be attached until they near the next area of detail when this closer work can be taken up again. These steps should be repeated until the design is complete.

Small seeds

Applying small seeds to the design can prove difficult, especially if the seeds are handled with the thumb and forefinger. A seed dispenser will prove invaluable in this case and will allow the seeds to be placed into position accurately and neatly. A liberal quantity of seeds must be discharged, more than in fact appears to be necessary. Press the seeds carefully into the glue with the guiding stick to settle them evenly, making sure that the area of glue is well covered. After the glue has hardened, a soft-haired painting brush may be used to wipe away loose seeds.

Fig. 12 The use of a seed dispenser will allow you to place small seeds in position as neatly and cleanly as possible.

Laying seeds *en masse* will require practice, especially when some of the shapes to be covered are intricate.

Large seeds

Larger seeds are handled more easily and can be placed into their positions with the thumb and fore-

Fig. 13 Large seeds can be handled more easily and placed into position with thumb and forefinger.

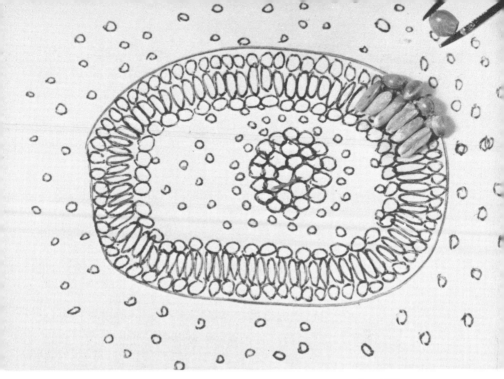

finger, or with the aid of tweezers.

Do not rush the seed-laying operation. True success demands patience and care and hurried work will give disappointing results.

Fig. 14 Tweezers are an invaluable asset in laying large seeds.

Fig. 15 The seeds in this study were placed into their position individually.

Experimenting

In previous chapters, we have mentioned the desirability of acquiring some experience in working with seeds before actually embarking on a picture. In this section, we have given some specific experiments relating to colour, texture and other materials apart from seeds which can be used to make up a seed mosaic.

Colour

Often the most suitable colour combinations in seeds are not always the most obvious. Try laying several small squares of seeds, for example lentils, and surround each square with a different coloured seed, for example, (*a*) Dutch blue maw, (*b*) niger and (*c*) sunflower. Now observe which surrounding colour shows up the lentils to greatest advantage. This can be done at any time by simply spreading the seeds on a card before a colour decision is made.

Try also to work out a shade card with the different seeds laid out from light to dark and stuck down. This could begin at one end with rice and finish at the other end with niger with other available seeds ranged in between. One must be careful here, however, as colour and tone are not the same thing. The best way

Fig. 16 A graded tonal chart ranging from very dark to very light. *Left to right*: black rape, red rape, linseed, jack millet, pin-head oatmeal and rice.

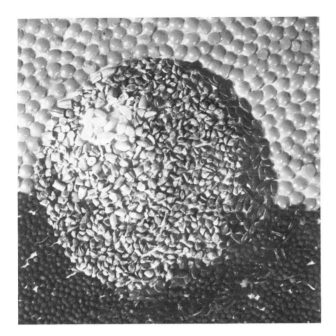

Fig. 17 A spherical form. Note the highlights and shadows which provide the shape.

Fig. 18 A cube. Again, note the different tones of the seeds giving shape and shadow.

to judge the tone of a seed is to half close one's eyes while making a comparison with other seeds. This cuts down the colour distraction and enables the light/dark value to stand out. One may ask why this tonal effect needs to be considered at all and indeed there is no necessity while one is dealing only in flat, stylized images. When, however, one begins to make some attempt at suggesting the dimensional form, for example in a head, then a tone chart will be found invaluable. An amusing exercise in tone is to try to build up the form of a ball or a box using suitable seeds to suggest shadows and highlights. (*See* Figs. 17 & 18.)

Textures and reliefs

Apart from the colours of seeds, which make picture making so enjoyable, each seed variety has its own characteristic shape. Many seeds are spherical but naturally each variety has a different size. For instance, one can build up pleasant, bubbly textures by laying a close area of split peas flat side down, or lentils flat side down. Both these seeds are basically hemi-spherical (when split) but the textures they make are individual due to their difference. It is sometimes easier to judge a texture by feeling it with the finger-tips rather than looking at it. A variation in texture can be achieved with the same seeds by adding some whole dried peas to the split ones, by mixing lentils and peas to achieve a less predictable surface, or by laying them edgewise.

Figs. 19 and 20 Two ordered patterns using peas and lentils.

One may see from this that we are now beginning to consider the seed picture as a type of bas relief. Adding this new quality lends a new dimension to the picture besides giving us many more effects to extend our image. For instance, sunflower seeds, when laid on their edges and overlapped horizontally or vertically, give us a strong, spiky effect. This is even more noticeable if they are set in the glue sitting on the blunt end so that the points are directed outwards. We must take care, however, that they do not become too dominant, for instance by using them in large quantities on a ground of small seeds. (*See* Figs. 24(a), (b) and (c).

These are only a few suggestions for possible textures. There are innumerable combinations of seeds which may be used to provide texture and the ingenious use of these will assist the composition. We have observed a tendency among students using seeds for the first time to ignore the possibilities of texture. It is not enough to rely solely on the accidental textural qualities of the seeds, even though the results can be pleasing. It is advisable to have at one's command a vocabulary of textures which can be employed where necessary. An experiment could be carried out by laying small areas of different seeds and then relating their textures to other things, for example, marigold gives a curly effect similar to hair, and sunflower seeds

Fig. 21 Haphazard arrangement of peas and lentils.

Fig. 22 Split peas set edgeways.

Fig. 23 Seeds used in relief give a very pleasing effect.

Allied materials

laid in a haphazard, spiky manner can simulate the leaves of a tree or shrub. (*See* Fig. 24(c).)

There are many other materials, similar in character to seeds, which may be used to supplement and extend the range of textures and patterns. These may be drawn from several separate sources. One may search the supermarket and harvest a collection of dried foodstuffs such as tapioca, sago and pasta in all its various shapes and sizes; the haberdashery can supply a wide range of beads; and the greengrocery offers nuts, shelled and unshelled.

Apart from the above materials which closely resemble seeds, there is no reason why, if the occasion demands, one should not apply materials which have no relationship at all. These elements could include drawing and mapping pins, buttons, drinking straws,

everlasting and pressed flowers. The list is endless, limited only by the ingenuity of the student.

There comes a point when working with seeds in relief when it is restricting to simply glue the seeds flat on to a baseboard. One may pile up the seeds until they reach out from the baseboard, or one may so mould the baseboard with wood or card that it is already in relief before the seeds are applied to the surface. It is logical from here to consider using the seeds three-dimensionally to produce small sculptures.

Figs. 24(a), (b) and (c) Three ways of laying sunflower seeds. The mood of each arrangement is quite different.

Sculptures

Fig. 25 A mixture of beads and buttons in haphazard arrangement. Compare this with Fig. 2, p. 11.

7 Looking for ideas

The search for subject matter is a very complex thing. There are so many sources upon which we may draw, that it depends entirely upon the taste, interests and environment of the reader. It may be that you have no problem at all and in fact have an array of ideas to choose from. However, it is more likely that, the practical and experimental stages being over, the question of a subject for a 'finished' piece of work finds the mind blank. If this is your problem, we offer the following suggestions and hope that they will promote a number of concrete ideas. We feel that the medium of seeds presents such an opportunity for creative work that it would be a pity simply to copy some other artist's work, for example a painting, photograph or ancient motif. The result may be a competent piece of work, but to use seeds in this way is to lose any claim to originality.

To be creative, we must cast out all prejudice and many of our pre-conceived ideas. It is necessary to look around with fresh eyes and re-educate ourselves to see subject matter in all things around us. There may be a wealth of possibilities staring one in the face, while one sees only the most obvious. For instance we may pick out a beautiful bloom on a plant while missing entirely the fascination of the dead heads around it. We observe a bird sitting on a wall, but ignore the patterns of erosion and mould on the wall itself. How often do we notice in the jumble of a toolshed or a kitchen the possibilities of a unique still life? The point we wish to emphasize is that we have no desire to give our reader a neat list of 'things to do'. It is for him to examine his environment and observe the endless procession of pattern and shape around him. Not only natural objects such as tree bark, stones, rocks, insects, clouds or flowers offer themselves, but also man-made things such as buildings, furniture,

Fig. 26 Stacked pipes.
Fig. 27 Pattern with granite blocks and figure.
Fig. 28 A worn stone wall.

wrought ironwork, fabric, packages, food. A walk along any high street would offer a feast to the eye: the counterchange of colour in a greengrocery, the tangle of bicycles against a wall, the stack of drainpipes waiting to be laid, a composition of umbrellas in the rain, and so on. If you live by the sea, the pattern of light on waves and ripples may present a far more delightful prospect than the oft-portrayed scenic view of the harbour. Maybe it is necessary to observe from a different viewpoint. It is remarkable how different the world appears when you look up or down at it. An unpicturesque town may create an unbelievable pattern when viewed from the church tower, and equally the silhouettes of rooftops could be far more remarkable than what is at ground level.

If we are still not settled on a theme, it may be of interest to 'go microscopic'. By this we mean that objects which do not in themselves appeal may have parts within them which provide a basis on which to work. For instance, instead of portraying a butterfly we may prefer to draw only on the patterns from its wings. It may or may not be necessary to actually magnify the object but many things achieve a new dimension under a microscope. Ordinary vegetable

Fig. 29 A butterfly.

matter, soil, skin and hair show their worth as subjects when viewed in magnification. Many medical or biological books have illustrations showing magnified cells etc. which are a wonder of abstract shape and form. Snowflakes, crystals, bugs and minute insects are all different when enlarged. It is not essential to have a means of enlarging things although this is enjoyable. All the above mentioned objects, and many more, may be found in scientific textbooks.

Sometimes it gives a refreshing new outlook on life if we look at it indirectly through reflections. A face reflected in a dark window may give a far more mysterious and ethereal image than one seen in a mirror, and the views thrown back from shop windows clash strangely with the objects within. The distortions which we may receive from polished surfaces are often amusing and a fine way of breaking with pre-conceptions. Observe yourself reflected from the back or front of a polished spoon, or notice how the kitchen appears as seen in the side of a kettle. It is necessary only to pick out the reflected information, not to draw also the object which is doing the reflecting unless this is desired. Not even the most insignificant object should be ignored for there is nothing which cannot be drawn upon to form the basis for a picture.

It may be that you will choose to work not from natural or man-made forms but from such things as geometric shapes or patterns and textures inspired by the seeds themselves. Many fascinating compositions may be arrived at by simply arranging the various shapes and colours of seeds and allowing them to dictate the structure of the picture. It would be impossible for us to attempt the task of setting out all the approaches and materials for inspiration. It is not for us to say what will be the spark that sets the reader off. As we said at the beginning of this chapter, we acknowledge the personal nature of subject choice and realize that we can only recommend to the reader a general direction in which to move.

8 Step by step through the colour illustrations

We have given, in the previous pages, a guide to the mechanics of creating a seed picture and the techniques of interpreting a design. It is hoped that, from the information given, the reader may embark, with confidence, on a picture of his own. However, we are aware that sometimes there is some difficulty in bridging the gap between reading about techniques, and interpreting them into a design. The barrier may be either in the search for a subject, or in the difficulty of where to begin or even in what seeds may be used for what purpose. For this reason we have decided to give the reader an insight into the creation of the colour plates in this book. It is hoped that these case histories, in showing the development of these pictures, will demonstrate how the techniques can be applied. The reader should not take these suggestions as the only way in which a picture may be produced.

'Portrait of Roger'
(10 in. × 13 in.—
25·4 cm. × 33·0 cm.)
by Glenda Marsh

The search for subject matter is, as mentioned in the section on design, a very personal thing. However, as a general rule, the more decorative the subject the better. Seeds obviously are not as flexible as paint but more akin to mosaic or embroidery. Therefore in many ways the subject must be simplified right from the beginning. In setting out to do a portrait of Roger, I took on a subject which was by no means easy. It is quite a simple thing to create a picture of a bird or an exotic fish using a photograph as a guide, but a normal, not very colourful, human being is another matter. The first step was to make a pencil drawing to try to capture a likeness, and more important to find out wherein the aspects of likeness lay. With any kind of portrait it is far too easy to lose the character mysteriously for no apparent reason. In fact I made two pencil drawings as the first proved to be a little small for my purpose. It is far easier to carry out the details of a seed picture if they are not too tiny. I quickly decided that the most recognizable aspects of Roger were his hair, which formed a dark cap, and

Plate 3 (*above*) 'Seed panel' (*see* p. 52)

Plate 4 (*below*) 'Geranium leaf variations' (*see* p. 53)

Plate 5 'Landscape' (see p. 54)

the dark shadows under his rather deepset eyes. Working on a piece of thick, white card approximately 10 in. × 13 in. (25·4 cm. × 33·0 cm.) I laid down a basis for the portrait and marked out the various areas of colour change, shadows and highlights, etc.

I began with the hair. At first I was somewhat stuck on the decision of what seeds to use in order to show up the highlights and also describe the shape of the head. After some experiment I found that sunflower seeds were ideal. I picked out the ones which had a dark brown or light brown colouring, a number of which had light stripes. The seeds were cut in half in order to make them lay smoothly and the stripes of the seeds enabled me to show the direction of hair growth. At the sides of the head I began at the bottom and worked upwards so that the seeds overlapped each other downwards as hair does. I found the best way to handle the sunflower seeds was to hold them with tweezers, stroke them across the glue brush and then lay them individually.

After the hair I tackled the face. It is difficult to treat a face decoratively without sacrificing any idea of a likeness and so I decided to use the seeds for their colour value on the face without too much considera-tion of surface pattern. I selected several types of seeds of a similar size but of colours varying from white to dark ochre. When using small seeds, it is a temptation to lay a large area of glue and shovel the seeds on, shaking away the excess, which is wasteful. I forwent the use of a seed dispenser on this occasion as the areas of colour change were quite small and would have necessitated a too frequent emptying of the container, and laid the glue in very small areas of approximately ½ in. (1·3 cm.) square, scattering the seeds in pinches and pressing them well into the glue with the back of my tweezers. The glue was spread with a small strip of flexible plastic ¼ in. (0·6 cm.) wide.

It seemed simplest to work from the eyes down-wards. Rice was used for the whites of the eyes as these were the lightest parts on the face. The eyelids were done in pin-head oatmeal and so was the forehead, as this was a medium-light area. Jack millet proved ideal for the deep shadows around the eyes as it was dark in contrast to the white rice, and it also proved useful for most of the other facial shadows as it was not too hard in colour. Dutch blue maw formed the irises of the eyes and black rape the pupils, and for a lively effect I added a small piece of chalky rice to each iris. The eyelashes and eyebrows were formed with black niger, a seed about $\frac{1}{4}$in. (0·6 cm.) long and these were added individually with tweezers on top of the seeds already laid. For the main areas of the face, pearl white millet was used for the light areas and panicum for the darker ones. It is not always apparent from close to whether the tones are correct or not. It is necessary to stand the picture up and observe from a distance the relationship of one area to another. At a distance the seeds are seen more as a colour or a tone and less as individual seeds.

If it becomes necessary, in the event of an incorrect tone being applied, to remove an area of seeds, caution must be exercised. I was using one of the plastic types of glue which is quite easy to remove by rubbing when dry. However, when I tried to remove a small area of seeds unsuitably placed, I found that not only the glue I had just laid was coming off but that it was also bringing with it another area of seeds. The glue had formed a continuous skin beneath all the seeds and as I pulled one edge it affected the surrounding areas. It would be quite easy to ruin hours of patient work in this manner, and I suggest running a sharp kraft knife blade between the area to be removed and those areas surrounding to cut out the portion of glue before stripping it off.

The facial structure was quite straightforward to build up using the three tones of pearl white millet, panicum and jack millet. The mouth proved something of a problem as there was only one seed of a suitable colour and this was a little too colourful, however I exercised artistic licence and used gold of pleasure for the lips with Dutch blue maw to add form and niger to separate them.

Having avoided the use of pattern in the face I allowed myself the pleasure of using the seeds more formally in the background. A pleasant, flowery effect was achieved on the shirt with paddy rice laid in star formation. This kind of seed-laying takes a long time as each seed must be handled individually with tweezers. On the areas of the walls the various seeds (oatmeal, jack millet and pearl barley) were laid with consideration of their variation in surface texture rather than colour. Lentils were used to give a splash of brilliance in the window. It was found when laying seeds such as Dutch linseed and niger that they could be picked up individually by touching them with tweezers which had a trace of glue on the tips. Then, when applied to the area of glue on the picture, the greater quantity of glue detached them from the tweezers. This was a convenient way of laying rather awkward seeds. Unfortunately, the same method cannot be used for seeds which are either very small or very large. Red and black rape, which are almost spherical, are extremely difficult to lay as they roll about freely and their spherical nature gives a very small point of contact with the baseboard. When the picture was complete, it was checked over and any small gaps where seeds had become detached were filled in with the appropriate seed. Finally a coat of polyurethane varnish was applied. (*See* Chapter 9.)

One of the most interesting points about this picture is that it was completed in 1963. This will dispel any fears that seed pictures have a short life. To date we have not had the experience of watching any of our seed pictures germinate! Neither has this work suffered in any way from mould or discoloration.

The inspiration for this subject was a 19th-century

'Period piece'
(15 in. × 9½ in.—
38·1 cm. × 24·1 cm.
by Roger Marsh

fashion plate showing the rear view of a woman wearing a bustle. The figure was surrounded with a strictly formalized border in the manner of a Victorian sampler. This work is an ideal example of how economical seed pictures can be, for it was carried out completely with one pound of parrot seed mixture from a pet shop and a packet of pudding rice. Although this was much cheaper than buying separate quantities of various seeds, it did entail the somewhat laborious and painstaking task of separating the seeds into different types. It was a simple matter to extract the sunflower seeds and the maize, but to separate the others it was helpful to place them in small amounts on a piece of paper and then tap gently underneath, causing the round seeds to separate out from the rest.

The picture was worked on a piece of hardboard which gave it a sepia appearance and brought out the period theme. The figure was drawn to scale and then traced on to the board. The border, however, was drawn direct. Most emphasis was placed on the shapes and patterns, with even the figure simplified into stripes, indicating the material of the dress. Rice was used to give a strong white contrast behind the figure, which was done mainly in black rape and yellow millet, seeds of a similar shape and size.

'Seed panel'
(6 in. × 9½ in.—
15·2 cm. × 24·1 cm.)
by Roger Marsh

I have always found when making seed pictures that while handling the seeds many new ideas for textures and patterns arise which do not necessarily fit into the picture I am working on. It is quite frustrating to have in one's hand beautiful seeds for which there is no immediate application. This seed panel was in some respects a self indulgence, a chance to use some of the decorative seeds we have collected but which had not all found places in our pictures. I divided the board into forty squares and simply filled these in ways which pleased me. The only limitations which I imposed were that neighbouring squares should not end up too similar in tone or texture. I did not restrict myself to one kind of seed per square but built them up and mixed them as required. The majority of seeds on this panel can be recognized from our classification chart (*see* pp. 12-19). However, the bottom left-hand square is worthy of note. These are 'popcorn' maize which were cooked in butter but not heated sufficiently to 'pop'. The result was a rich golden brown seed with a black spot and a much rounder form than the original maize. The melon seeds third from the right at the top have been dyed green with food colouring and it is observable how out of sympathy this green is with the natural greens of the peas and coffee beans. It may not be evident from this colour plate, but much of this picture is raised well above the surface of the card. The peas, for instance, on the right are built into a pyramid which projects 1 in. (2·5 cm.) above the card, and the cherry pips second row third from left merely sit on a background of rice seeds. One would normally have thought that projections such as these would render the picture fragile, but this picture was finished with a coat of clear polyurethane varnish which, apart from glossing the seeds, has the effect of bonding them all together with a continuous 'skin'.

This particular illustration was produced with a view to showing how an original sketch from any subject can be carried on to a finished piece of work. The drawing was made from the nearest subject to hand, which happened to be a pot of geraniums, and then squared up to a usable size (*see* Figs. 9 (a) and (b). The most noticeable features of the geranium leaves were the pink and green veins on the undersides which were visible because this plant had grown straggly. I attempted to keep this veined appearance throughout the illustration as it seemed to me to be the most interesting feature of the drawing along with the variation in size of leaf.

I began quite objectively with the largest leaf,

'Geranium leaf variations'
(10 in. × 7 in.— 25·4 × 17·8 cm.)
by Glenda Marsh

attempting to portray the veined and mottled appearance by sticking down unroasted coffee beans and gunga peas. However, by the time that I came to the outer edge, which I defined with bright green split peas and grey-green hemp, it was obvious that an unexpected atmosphere was developing. The geranium leaves were quite delicate in their colour variation and veining, whereas the seed version was of an entirely different character. It reminded me strongly of lollipop trees and other such fairytale vegetation. I decided to interpret the rest of the picture with this fantasy aspect in mind. I therefore abandoned the colour scheme which I had premeditated and did the two lowest leaves in orange lentils with green split pea outlines. The veins looked satisfactorily spidery using patna rice. The leaf at the top left is made up of yellow split peas and lentils, a paler tone to throw forward the dark central leaf. I enjoyed the top right-hand leaf perhaps most of all, using varying sizes of red beans to portray the leaf sections. The red beans look so like jelly beans that they fitted straight into the new character of the picture. I made all the stalks stiff with regularly placed contrasting coloured seeds to carry on the lollipop idea. In order that the background should in no way interfere, I made it neutral in colour while treating each of the spaces between the leaves as a different area and varying the textures. The final result was a pleasing and colourful piece of work bearing little relationship to the original neglected pot of geraniums.

'Landscape'
(17 in. × 14 in.—
43·2 × 35·6 cm.)
by Roger Marsh

With a landscape as with any other subject matter the nature of the seeds will stamp its unmistakable characteristic on the picture. One is forced to interpret the subject into the language of seeds and the subject does not necessarily lose in the translation. It is a mistake to try to stick too closely to the original theme without allowing the seeds to control the result. After all, it is the original effect of the seeds which differentiates this medium from any other. This landscape is a good example of this point. We usually think of a landscape as being predominantly green and brown. However, as we have observed previously in this book, green is not a common colour among mature seeds, though brown obviously is. Consequently a decision was taken to carry out this subject in a natural brown, gold and black colour scheme, natural, that is, to the seeds. The result is a brilliantly coloured composition which, although the colours may seem somewhat unusual, for instance in the sky, is quite acceptable as a landscape. Indeed I feel that through allowing the seeds to dictate the choice of colour they have made a valuable contribution to the work. They seem to have captured more than I had originally planned.

Apart from the colour aspect, I had to be selective in the shapes which I chose to express the landscape. The trees were first drawn very simply while trying not to lose any of their fascinating intricacies of shape. The sky also was resolved into large shapes indicating cloud formations. The ploughed field was shown by simple lines in perspective. All of this was necessary, of course, before seed-laying could begin. I used a cement-type glue for this picture, and it was carried out on thick card with the help of a seed applicator. Only five different seed varieties were used. These were panicum, mazagan canary, gold of pleasure, Dutch linseed and niger. Panicum was used as a basis for the sky and also to give a bright background against which to place the tree silhouettes. The trees were carried out in combinations of gold of pleasure, linseed and niger. Linseed and niger are particularly convincing for the trees as they give a leafy appearance to the outline when laid freely. These two also were used to define the ploughed field and give it a suitably earthy look. (*See also* Figs. 8(a) and (b).)

9 Varnishing, mounting and framing

When a seed picture has been completed, it should be left for the glue to harden thoroughly. The longer the time allowed for this process the better, but a few days should see this through. The picture at this point can be considered finished, but we recommend that the picture is given one or two thin coats of polyurethane varnish to protect the seeds. A coat of varnish will also bond the seeds firmly together, bring up their colours and help to prevent discoloration by bright sunlight. There are, however, one or two disadvantages in using varnish. White seeds, for example, are subject to discoloration, and if too much varnish is applied, it can take on the property of toffee.

We have found the clear gloss polyurethane varnishes to be the most successful, but we would like to point out that there are varnishes which are matt and a range which have staining properties. Care should be exercised when using any varnish from this group, for the result obtained may not be the one expected and can spoil or even ruin one's work. A test should be made by laying a strip of varnish upon a card of seeds prepared specifically for this purpose using the same range of seeds employed in the finished picture. This simple procedure will prevent any nasty shocks, or reveal any pleasing effects.

Fig. 30 Floating seeds should be removed with tweezers.

There is also a clear spray varnish available in a pressurized can, which may also be used.

Place the picture face up on top of several sheets of newspaper and inspect the work for 'floating', loose seeds, seeds missing, and any foreign matter. Floating seeds should be removed with tweezers, a soft brush, or needle; seeds that are missing from their positions can easily be replaced; and any unwanted bits and pieces which have settled on the design (for example, hair, crumbs, hard glue particles), can be taken away using the same method as for floating seeds.

Using a 1-in. (2·5-cm.) or 2-in. (5·1-cm.) brush, lay a thin film of varnish over the entire picture area. The brushing action is a combination of lightly stroking over the surface of the seeds, and dabbing gently down with the tip of the brush to place the varnish between the crevices. One coat may quite easily be sufficient, but a second will cause no harm; this should be applied after the first coat is thoroughly dry.

Fig. 31 Varnishing with poly-urethane varnish. Stroke the brush gently over the seeds and dab down gently with the tip.

Varnishing with clear gloss poly-urethane

57

Always throw away the newspaper after use, and immediately clean the brush in the solvent recommended by the varnish manufacturers.

Varnishing with clear varnish spray   A little preparation is required before the varnish spray can be used.

The picture to be sprayed can either be laid flat or stood upright. Whichever position is decided upon a liberal covering of newspaper should be placed all the way around the spray area. The spray area may be sited indoors or, if it is a still, calm, warm day, outside. To help contain the spray within a manageable area, a spray bay can be made. If the picture is small enough, all that is required to produce this is a large cardboard box. Cut off the card flaps at the top of the box and lay the box down on its side; then prop up the picture inside the box.

When spraying indoors, make sure that the room is well ventilated. Detailed spraying instructions will, of course, be given on the side of the can, but as a general rule the picture should be sprayed from a distance of about one foot. It is advisable to spray on several very thin layers, gradually building up the required finish rather than one heavy, thick coat.

Allow time for the varnish to harden before proceeding with the mounting and framing operations.

Mounting your picture   The most suitable way to present seed pictures is to mount and/or frame them. The decision of which method to adopt is personal, and there are of course economic considerations. The following are three alternative methods.

Surface mounting   This involves taking a piece of flat, surfaced board, for example hardboard or plyboard (something reasonably firm) and gluing the seed picture flat upon its surface. The size of the mounting board should be the same proportions as the picture, and approximately one-third larger than the picture's dimension. This

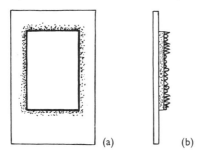

will allow a margin of 'ground' board to project
around the outside edge of the work. Having cut the
board to size, place the picture upon the board to
determine its final position. It is advisable to keep the
margins on the left and right sides equal, and the
margin at the bottom slightly larger than the margin
at the top. (*Note:* pictures to be surface mounted
should be worked without a $\frac{1}{4}$ in. (o·6 cm.) margin
around their perimeter.)

A pencil dot may then be placed at the four corners
of the picture on the board to mark its position, or, if
necessary, a thin, light pencil line can be drawn around
the picture edge. At this point the margins can be
varnished or, if preferred, painted with a household
paint. Choice of colour is important because an
unwisely chosen colour could be detrimental to the
picture. It is a fairly safe assumption that white, grey
or a neutral colour will enhance the picture without
demanding all the attention. Brighter colours do have
their place, but only on certain occasions, and are the
exception rather than the rule.

All is now ready for the picture to be glued to the
board. This can be done quite satisfactorily by using
an impact adhesive.

Window or aperture mounting

In this instance the picture to be mounted is placed
behind a piece of card in which a window has been
previously cut. The size of the card should be as
mentioned above, approximately one-third larger than

59

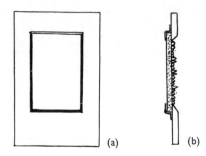

Figs. 33(a) and (b) Window
mounting, front and side views.

(a)

(b)

the size of the seed picture. This size will give a
satisfying result, but is entered here only as a guide.
The reader may feel that a size larger or perhaps
smaller would be more apt. Card can be purchased in
a variety of colours, and the sentiments expressed
above apropos of colour, apply here too. A window
has now to be cut in the card.

First, its size and position must be marked. The
size will be fractionally larger than the seed picture
itself (less than $\frac{1}{4}$ in.—0·6 cm.)

Once the size of the window is known, it must be
positioned and marked out on the card. There are in fact
many different positions in which a window may be
placed in a piece of mounting card, but for simplicity,
we have described a widely accepted formula for
mounting single pieces of work. We recommend the
same proportions as given for surface mounting; i.e.
that the margins to the left and right are equal and
the margin at the bottom is a little bigger than that at
the top. The window size can be transferred to the
card by cutting out a shape of paper (brown or newspaper will suffice) to the same dimensions as the
picture, and laying it upon the card. After a few
adjustments, and a check with a rule, the paper pattern
can be soon positioned. This done, a thin, light pencil
line drawn around the pattern will complete the job,
and the window can be cut out. Care should be taken
when cutting out the window that the kraft knife is
sharp and a cutting board is placed beneath the card.

When the window has been cut, and the appropriate piece of card removed, the mount is placed over the seed picture. If it was measured and cut accurately the card will fit snuggly, not pressing too tightly against the seeds, or fitting so loosely that the edges of the baseboard can be seen through the window.

The mount can be secured to the picture either with adhesive tape for a temporary fixture, or with glue, which will bond the mount and the picture together permanently.

Framing

A seed picture may be framed unmounted, with the seeds situated directly next to the frame, or mounted and then framed. The job of framing can be placed into the hands of a professional frame-maker or the work may be undertaken at home or under the guidance of a teacher.

The standard of framing by frame-makers varies enormously, so it is always a good policy to be aware of the standard of workmanship before placing an order with a particular concern.

If one has the facility of a school or college and the guidance of a teacher, there is no reason why a first-class piece of work should not be produced. The same result can also be achieved in the home workshop, with perhaps the help of a friend. Whatever one's circumstances are, there is no point in setting out to make a picture frame unless one intends, at the very least, to make a good job of it. A seed picture which

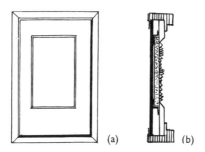

(a)   (b)

Figs. 34(a) Window mount and frame and (b) with backboard.

Figs. 35(a) Frame and (b) frame with backboard.

(a)

(b)

has taken a great deal of thought, time and patience to produce deserves to be well framed.

Whichever method one decides upon, a choice of framing material has to be made. We all have our own preferences and it would be unwise to be adamant in suggesting any particular framing material. However, as a guide, a frame that is sympathetic to the colouring of the seeds, usually proves to be the most successful. We find natural unpainted wooden frames a pleasant accompaniment to the various tones of the seeds.

Seeds may be purchased locally from bird seed **Suppliers**
merchants, grocery stores, supermarkets or gardening
shops, etc. The seeds can also be obtained by preserving
them at home. (*See* p. 20)

However, if a reader has difficulty in obtaining bird **Seeds**
seed, the authors are able to supply a wide range of bird
seed by mail. Please send a stamped, self-addressed
envelope for price list to:

Mr. and Mrs. R. Marsh, Ironstone Cottage, Church
Street, Nettleton, Lincoln, Lincolnshire, LN7 6NP.

Generally speaking almost all of the materials **Materials**
required can be bought from a local supplier, but
should this prove to be difficult or inconvenient, the
following addresses may be helpful:

Dryad, Northgates, Leicester, LE1 4QR.

Margros, Monument House, Monument Way
West, Woking, Surrey.

George Rowney & Co., Ltd., P.O. Box 10,
Bracknell, Berkshire, RG12 4ST.

Reeves and Sons Ltd., Lincoln Road, Enfield,
Middlesex.

Windsor and Newton, Educational Division,
Wealdstone, Harrow, Middlesex.

Index The figures in bold refer to the colour plates

64